THE
DIFFERENCE
MAKER

A SIMPLE FABLE ABOUT MAKING A DIFFERENCE IN THE LIFE OF OTHERS

The Difference Maker
Copyright © 2013 by Tony Bridwell
Published by B2B Books

ISBN: 0615811744
ISBN 13: 9780615811741
Library of Congress Control Number: 2013909288
B2B Books, Flower Mound, Texas

Library of Congress Cataloging-in-Publication Data

Printed in the United States of America

12 13 14 15 16 / 5 4 3 2 1

THE
DIFFERENCE
MAKER

A SIMPLE FABLE ABOUT MAKING A DIFFERENCE IN THE LIFE OF OTHERS

TONY BRIDWELL

ACKNOWLEDGMENTS

It is predawn as I sit in my office contemplating the acknowledgments page of my first book. With my trusty mug of coffee and my faithful dogs, Maddie and Westly, the only other brave souls to be awake at this hour, I begin to list those I need to thank.

As I look over my notes, it becomes obvious within the first few keystrokes that the pages required to acknowledge everyone who has made an impact on my life and this book would rival the pages of the book itself. Given that, I feel there should be a standard disclaimer for all acknowledgment pages—"For everyone I've forgotten, thank you!"

There are a few people, however, I must acknowledge for their (at times unknowing) contributions to my life and the life of this book—for example the members of the

Bible study class I lead on Sunday mornings. Without their longsuffering willingness to endure my teaching, much of what I've written never would have found its way to these pages. Our journey through God's word together over the last eight years has revealed every nugget of truth printed between the covers of this book.

I also should acknowledge my family, beginning with my bride, Dee. She has become my inspiration on more than one occasion as I have watched her become a difference maker in the lives of those close to her. For more than twenty-three years, she has made a daily difference in my life.

Allison, aka "Sis," has been my sounding board since she was old enough to sit up on her own. Her willingness to listen to story after story and provide real-time feedback has filled my soul with joy for years. Her keen design intuition led to the cover graphics and logos. Our Saturday-morning breakfast talks are true treasures in my life.

Ultimately this book would not have seen the light of day without my son Brendan. Through our relationship I realized the importance of being an active father and the increasingly important need of mentors in the lives of future generations. Brendan has encouraged me—in ways he may never fully understand—to draw closer to the Heavenly Father in order to draw closer to Brendan. For that I am forever grateful.

Finally anyone who knows me understands my limited but adequate Oklahoma education, which makes applying words correctly on paper a challenge on a good day. This project would not have made it to print if not for the extraordinary work of my editor and writing coach Nicole. Her spirit-led insights breathed life into every character within the pages of this story. She has a God-given talent.

It seems almost certain there is someone I am leaving out. As a matter of fact, I am sure of it. So for everyone I've forgotten, thank you!

FOREWORD

To paraphrase the great American philosopher Merle Haggard, "The first time I met Tony Bridwell is a favorite memory of mine." I was a new staff member at our church, and Tony was the teacher of a young single-adult class. I was immediately struck with the warm enthusiasm and genuine caring he showed for all the members of the class, as well as his love for teaching the word of God. I soon learned that Tony was the same guy every Sunday and that he was just as encouraging and supportive in private. We began what is now a fifteen-year friendship.

Over numerous rounds of golf, many meals, and hours of conversation, I have grown to admire and respect Tony's heart for his helping others and for his desire to make a difference in the lives of his family, friends, and anyone who will let him. He still teaches Sunday school to a packed crowd at his church (they had to move to a larger room to accommodate more people), and he still has the same enthusiasm and encouraging spirit. And the Lord has allowed Tony to be an encourager to hundreds of businesses and thousands of corporate executives around the world. His success proves that both he and his message are the real deal.

This book represents the heart of Tony's philosophy of life—to make a difference in the lives of others by pointing them to a deeper walk with the Lord and encouraging them to go deeper in discipleship. Through Brendan's journey through the journals of Taylor Bellows, Tony reminds us of how our potential for positive influence is always present, even if we don't think we're making a difference in the lives of others.

He also reminds us that, as our mentors influence us, we can in turn become mentors as well as positive influences in the lives of others. This pay-it-forward concept is more than just a kind word or deed offered; it's also a lifestyle that is effective in making permanent and significant differences in the lives of family, friends, and coworkers. I think this is what Tony means when he challenges us to be *all in*; our influence is a 24-7 proposition, and our influence is more powerful when it is consistent and constant.

One of the greatest needs of the human heart is encouragement. Just when we need them, the Lord brings into our lives those who bring encouragement, support, and words of affirmation. Tony Bridwell is such a person, a modern-day Barnabas who is a difference maker in the lives of many. This book is his encouragement to help you be a difference maker in your sphere of influence.

—*Joe Cook, PhD, Dallas Baptist University*

Chapter One
THE DIARY

Rain. A fitting accompaniment to a dreary appointment with death. Brendan tugged the collar of his raincoat around his chin and shrugged his shoulders to shield more of his face against the wind. He reached behind him and shut his car door, then crossed the street, dodging the oncoming four-lane traffic that was quite the paradox for the historical district through which it flowed.

Brendan plodded up the creaky porch steps and entered the old two-story Cape Cod that, from the outside, usually made him nostalgic. But the only nostalgia he could muster was in longing for his best friend, Taylor Bellows, II. Brendan placed a foot on the bottom step of the antique staircase, one of the last remaining interior originals, and gazed up at the door to the converted office space. It seemed so far away. Brendan sighed, his energy buried with Taylor, and began the climb.

It was a wonder Mark Coleman never had taken the money the Bellows family had paid him for his legal services and moved his offices to a Manhattan high-rise with a doorman and an elevator. Didn't all lawyers aspire to such a New York City existence? Apparently Mark was one of the rare ones. Then again Brendan wouldn't have wanted that either. There was something to be said for a slower pace of life—smelling the roses and all that. If only Taylor could have caught on before…before it was too late.

A shoulder brushed his. "Oh. Excuse me." Brendan glanced up to lock eyes with Mark's young assistant. "I didn't see you there." How had he missed her? He shook his head to clear his thoughts. He needed to get it together.

"Mr. Austin…" Chelsea placed a hand on Brendan's forearm. "I am so sorry for the loss of Mr. Bellows."

Brendan sucked in a breath. It took him by surprise every time he heard it. Loss. Taylor. Gone. They'd been apart for weeks at a time before but always with the expectation that Taylor would be jetting in from some far-flung place any day or that he'd pull his head out of the boardroom for some recreation after the big contract was signed. Not this time.

Brendan offered a swift nod. "Thank you." Was he supposed to say more? What was left? Small talk would be impossible. Mercifully Chelsea moved away, down the stairs.

Finally, at the top of the stairs, Brendan paused with his hand on the bannister finial and took a deep breath. What he wouldn't give for a little dip of snuff. It was a nasty habit, and he would quit—he really would. After all he'd promised Taylor and Ann. Just not today. One day at a time.

Brendan approached the office door. Why had Mark asked him here? The will had been read days before. What remained for a lawyer to do after that? He placed his hand on the doorknob and paused. *Well, turn it*, he thought. He wasn't going to find answers as he stood in the hallway. A sense of dread shrouded Brendan's heart. But why? Taylor was gone; nothing he heard in that room could make it any truer. So the worst was over.

"Brendan, good to see you. Thanks for coming by." Mark turned the corner from the back stairway, his suit jacket peppered with raindrops. "Sorry I'm late. I'm between meetings. Come on in so we can catch up." He reached forward and turned the knob, then gestured Brendan in.

Brendan led the way to what once must have been the master bedroom of the old house, judging by the crown moldings and the bay window looking onto the busy street. Long ago that view would have been of horse-drawn carriages making their rickety way down the lane, along with people strolling by in their appropriate dress and parasols. Nothing good ever stayed the same.

Blinking against the fluorescent lights, a stark contrast to the dreary day, Brendan chose one of the mismatched mid-century side chairs. He lowered his body into it but sat at attention in front of a desk that easily could have been original to the house.

Ann would say Mark's tastes were eclectic—"shabby chic"—and she'd find a Pinterest board to prove it. A chuckle escaped before Brendan could stop himself. That assessment might have been true if Mark cared one iota about his decor, but in reality it was nothing more than an accident.

Mark nudged one of the chairs back a few inches and perched on the edge of his desk. He tipped his head toward Brendan and opened his mouth.

Here we go.

"Thanks for stopping by. You must be wondering why you're here." Mark grimaced. "Probably could have done without seeing me for a while, huh?"

"The thought had crossed my mind. I mean, the will's been read."

There couldn't possibly be more money to divide. Four hours of that the other day had been enough financial talk to last a lifetime—and enough actual money to last Brendan a lot of lifetimes, especially the way he and Ann lived. Oh, plus the B2B ranch, Taylor's hunting property. What more could Brendan need or want in this life? Besides his best friend?

"Look." Mark shrugged. "The reading the other day was an emotional time for all of us. That's why I thought it best that we meet privately for this part."

"Is everything OK?"

"Yes, it is. It's just that Taylor left something a bit… um, personal…that he wanted me to take care of should anything happen to him. It's…well…" Mark strode to the closet and slid open the bifold door to reveal three Bellows Corporation boxes. Mark heaved each box over to Brendan and dropped it with a thud at his feet, then slid back onto his perch on the desk.

Brendan stared at the boxes, not knowing what to think. "What's all this?"

"That's what you're here to find out." Mark nodded at the first box. "Take a look."

Brendan shifted in his chair and inched his hands toward the first box, his heart racing. What was he so afraid of? It wasn't like anything in that box was going to bite him. Then again the truth sometimes did bite. There was something in that box—something Taylor had once possessed that Brendan knew nothing about, something Taylor had shared with his attorney but not with Brendan.

Once Brendan opened that box, he would know something about his best friend he hadn't known just an hour ago, and he'd never be able to return to the moment when there were no secrets. Nothing good ever stayed the same.

Brendan lifted the lid and peered inside. The spines of what had to be more than a dozen black, leather-bound journals stared up at him from their neat row. They were the same kind of journals he and Taylor used to play with when they got stuck at Mr. Bellows's office. Taylor's father would run off on some business emergency to save or make a million dollars and leave the boys to occupy themselves.

Taylor would open one of those empty books and pretend he was a lawyer. Just then Brendan felt his heart smile, though his face probably didn't. He could see his friend lick the end of the pencil like lawyers did in old movies. Taylor would place a hand on the armrest of the chair where Brendan sat and stare into Brendan's eyes as he interrogated him for having committed one heinous crime after another. He built an imaginary case until even Brendan thought he was guilty.

Brendan shook his head and ran his hand through his hair. How many hours had they spent like that? Well, just as many as it took until Mr. Bellows returned a richer man and the boys could break free and get back outside to run through the woods and along the creek, as far away from the steel prison of Mr. Bellows's company as they could get.

Funny how Taylor had signed himself up for a life sentence at that same prison he'd once been so desperate to escape.

Brendan trailed his fingers over the years scrawled on the fine-leather spines. He slid out the previous year's volume and ran his palm over the front cover, then traced the gold-embossed engraving in the bottom-right corner— "David Taylor Bellows, II." Brendan slowly lifted the front cover as he glanced up at Mark.

"According to what Taylor said, these volumes collectively comprise his personal journals. Everything he ever did, said, or thought, he put into these books." Mark shook his head. "All three boxes are full."

As Brendan stared at the first page, the words blurred against the sting in his eyes. "I didn't even know he kept a diary. Best friends for forty years, and he never said a word to me about a diary." Had Brendan spoken aloud? The roar in his head drowned out the sound of the words.

"No one knew." Mark shrugged. "I worked as closely as anyone with Taylor, and he never let on he was keeping a personal record."

Not as close as me, Brendan thought. *Nowhere near.* "But these volumes have to have taken hundreds of hours of work. The time this took…" Brendan's stomach churned. How had he not known? More important, why hadn't Taylor trusted Brendan enough to let him in on what he was doing? Why the secrecy?

"Have you read any of this?" Brendan's eyes locked on the pages as he flipped through the book.

"Not one word. Couldn't bring myself to even open the boxes." Mark leaned back and reached for a slip of paper atop the stack in his inbox. "I did read this, though. Taylor wrote it some time ago—four years, to be exact." He held it out.

Brendan waved his hand. "What does it say?" No way could his eyes take letters and form them into words…and then words into sentences. No way.

Mark cleared his throat and read the letter aloud.

Mark,

We have been friends for a long time. I trust that, should anything ever happen to me, you will be there to complete my final wishes. In addition to the will you insisted on writing for me—for which I am convinced you charged me by the word—I want you to pass on something that is very valuable to me.

Since college I have written in a journal. It started out as a favor to my father. I thought I would fill just one journal and be done. But here I am, all these years later, and I am still writing. No one knows I've been keeping these, not even Allison. You will find them in my personal safe in my office. The combination is the date of my father's death. You should not have any trouble collecting them with this letter.

Please give the journals to Brendan.

Make sure Brendan knows that after all these years and the many trials and tribulations we have gone through, he is the only one I trust to read these. He has truly been a difference maker in my life, and I regret never having told him. Make sure he gets the complete set; he will know what to do with them. Thanks for your help.

Best regards,
Taylor

Brendan's breath caught as he slid from his chair and slumped to his knees. He clutched his hair as sobs wracked his body. *Taylor. Taylor.* He rocked back and forth. "Oh, God. I miss him so much." He sat back on his heels beside the boxes and shook his head. It was too much. "I can't do this." Tears poured from his eyes and landed in heavy drops on his shirt.

Mark nodded and held out a box of tissues. "I know, man. I know.

"How many are there?" Brendan's voice cracked.

"Twenty-three journals, I believe. I'll send them to your house this afternoon."

Brendan wiped his face. "Thanks."

"If you don't mind my asking, what do you think he meant when he said you would know what to do with them?" Mark said, as he examined one of the diaries.

"I haven't a clue."

"Just like Taylor to leave something vague and mysterious."

Brendan started to replace the lid but noticed one journal wasn't quite like the others; there was no date on it. He pulled it out and drew it nearer until he could read the inscription—*The Summary.*

"Wonder what this one's all about?" Brendan shifted the book so Mark could read the title.

Mark's shoulders hitched. "Seems like a good place to start."

Brendan opened the journal to the first page. He hadn't seen Taylor's once familiar scrawl since technology had afforded other options. He took a deep breath and read aloud from the journal. " 'I start this final journal as a summary of the leadership lessons I've learned on my journey.' " The date was precisely one year before Taylor's death.

Brendan thumbed through the gold-leafed pages that were filled with handwritten words—words from Taylor's heart.

It took Taylor an entire year to write *The Summary*? If it took a full year for him to summarize the contents of these journals, there was no telling what Brendan would find when he began reading. And—wait a second—how had Taylor known that he was at a place in his life when a *summary* of all he'd learned was in order?

Had Taylor known his days were numbered?

Brendan needed time. And privacy. He leaned back against his chair and looked up at Mark. "I think I'll take this one with me if that's OK. Can you have the rest sent to the cabin?"

Mark nodded. His lips formed the word "Sure," but no sound escaped.

"Thanks for everything, man. You're a good friend." Brendan stood and extended his arm as he blinked against the stinging in his eyes.

Mark grasped Brendan's hand and squeezed his shoulder. "Let me know if I can be of any further help. You know I'm here for you."

"I know. Thanks. For now I think I need sleep." It sounded good, but there would be no respite for Brendan that night. Or maybe ever.

Brendan walked out of the stately building and stood on the expansive wraparound porch. He peered through the sheets of rain toward his parked car, which was almost a block away. The journal would get soaked if he didn't do something. He slipped the book under his jacket then pulled up the zipper. Water-resistant? Hopefully it would live up to its claims. If only he'd brought his umbrella. A lot of good it did him tucked under the front seat. Well, he'd better make his move.

Stepping out from under the shelter of the porch, into the pouring rain, Brendan took long strides toward his car. Rain pelted his face, a biting reminder that he still took up space in the world. He was alive. The thought held little solace.

The urge to lift his face into the rain and let it drench him from head to toe threatened to overtake his good sense, but he'd sooner die than get that journal wet.

Finally he reached his hand out to grasp the door handle and pulled it toward him. He dove inside and collapsed into the driver's seat. As water dripped off Brendan's nose and eyelashes, he wasted no time before reaching up to the steering wheel and clicking the hands-free feature of his cell phone. After scrolling through his recent numbers, he touched "Send" when he came to the one for home. *Please answer. Please answer.*

Just hearing her voice would do him a world of good.

"Hi, sweetie. Where are you?"

Ah, Ann. Brendan rested against the headrest and let peace wash over him. Thirty years of marriage hadn't dulled the effect her voice had on him. It was like a hug from an angel.

"I'm just leaving Mark's office. Seems Taylor had a few other things he left me." How could he convey the weight of this discovery to Ann? She'd never understand the stirrings of longing and feelings of betrayal that danced in his heart like oil and water.

Ann remained silent for a few moments. "Are you going to tell me, hon?"

Brendan heaved a sigh. "Seems Taylor had a diary… well, more like volumes of journals."

The silence on the other side spoke louder than any words his wife could say. She was piecing it together, just like Brendan needed her to.

Ann cleared her throat. "OK. It's Friday night…"

Her tone was clipped, in that take-charge manner Brendan had come to rely on through the years. He almost could see her looking at her watch as her brain sorted through the options and his needs. Eyes closed, Brendan waited for his wife to fix everything, as he knew she would.

"Why don't you head up to the cabin? I'll give you a couple of days, and I'll join you there later this weekend."

Brendan smiled. That was his girl. His Ann. She wasn't a mindreader; she was simply in tune with God's leading. She knew God's heart, and Brendan reaped the rewards.

His shoulders sagged. Taylor never would have the chance to know a marriage like that. Taylor and Allison could have had a beautiful marriage, but his indiscretions had gotten in the way too many times for trust to take root and hold on. Brendan sighed at the memory of the multiple occasions he'd spent the night consoling his best friend over yet another misstep in his marriage. Yes, Taylor had been his best friend, but Allison didn't deserve the mistreatment she'd endured—not that she'd been perfect either. Just when they'd really started to find a place of healing, Taylor was gone. And now it was too late.

"You know, hon, that sounds like a great idea." Brendan turned the key in the ignition and flipped on the wipers. "I'm going now. I'll give you a call when I get there." He eyed the journal that lay on top of his packed duffel bag on the floor.

"Sounds good, love. Be careful. No reading and driving. Promise?"

How did she do that? "Promise. I love you."

Chapter Two
THE SUMMARY

The tires crunched the wet gravel as Brendan pulled up the tree-lined lane and approached the log cabin tucked away in the woods. It was nestled among the mountains, right at the foothills of heaven—the perfect getaway location. This weekend it was just right for a runaway.

He shivered as he stepped from his car and flung his duffel over his shoulder. The air had cooled during the hour-long drive to higher elevation, and the afternoon sky had deepened to ocean blue with the passing storms. He squinted into the distance. Were more storms on the way? Not that it mattered. The biggest one he'd have to weather wasn't abating any time soon.

First things first. Brendan trudged up the gray wooden steps to the rustic porch. He circled past the front door to the woodpile on the side of the house. Good thing he'd moved the stacks up to the porch or they'd be soaked from the rain. Brendan shivered as he laid down the leather pouch and filled it with various-size logs, the makings of a roaring fire. That and a cup of hot coffee, and he'd be ready to spend the afternoon reading—at least physically ready. Mentally? That was another question entirely.

He stepped through the door and dragged the heavy stack of wood across the family room, then opened the iron gate that blocked the front of the huge stone fireplace he'd added last year. "Just like one you'd find at a ski lodge," Ann had begged. Her wish had been Brendan's command. Every stone upon stone was a love offering to his wife.

The straps slid from his shoulders until the bag fell with a thump beside his favorite chair. He bent over and stacked the wood, Boy Scout style, inside the fireplace. He struck a match to a few pieces of cardboard and held the growing flame beneath the kindling. The sparks ignited, and Brendan watched as the bigger pieces of wood caught the fire from the tiny flames. Soon an orange flickering glow filled the cavern. His knees cracked and popped as he stood upright and rubbed his cold hands together. Warmth soon would overtake the chilly room.

Now for light. He strode to the picture window that faced the fireplace and threw open the heavy drapes. Though the day was overcast, natural light flooded the space. The lake at the edge of his yard rocked from the rain, its water a deep blue to match the sky. Brendan rested a palm at the top of the window frame and pressed his forehead against the icy glass, soothing a headache he hadn't realized he had. A couple of Tylenol to go with that coffee would do the trick.

He moved through the already warming room toward the galley kitchen in back. Maybe that would be his next project. Ann had said she didn't need anything more than what was already there. But wouldn't she love a brand-new kitchen? They definitely had the money for it now.

He reached into the chipped white cupboard above the old-fashioned percolator and retrieved the can of coffee. There would be no milk in the fridge, so the powdered stuff would have to do. His favorite I'D RATHER BE FISHING! coffee mug, a gift from Ann, stood in the dish drainer, where they'd left it drying a few weeks before. Maybe he and Ann could get some fishing in this weekend when she came.

Ugh. Enough stalling. Brendan stirred a spoonful of powdered creamer and the contents of a packet of Splenda into his coffee. Then he took a deep breath.

Now or never, he thought.

He shuffled from the kitchen to his beloved overstuffed leather chair. In a single, well-practiced motion, he set his coffee down, plopped into the chair, and kicked up the leg rest.

Brendan reached into his bag beside the chair and retrieved *The Summary*. Placing it gently in his lap, he lifted his coffee mug and let the steam bathe his face. He took a warm sip and allowed the heat to flow through his body. With nothing more to delay the inevitable, he lifted the cover and blinked away the moisture that made the words swim.

I start this journal as a summary of the leadership lessons I've learned along the way.

Those were the words that had been stuck in his head since he had left Mark's office. As Brendan turned the page, he settled deep into his chair and began to read and relive the life of D. Taylor Bellows, II.

Chapter Three
TRUE SUCCESS

If this is success, I should have opted for failure.

Huh. Brendan sipped his coffee. That was an odd state-ment coming from one of the wealthiest men in the world, especially to start off a book about leadership.

> *In thinking back to what first impacted my life, I trailed through my history, all the way to my college years when Father would meet Brendan and me for lunch. We felt so adult walking into Bubba's to hang out with my dad. Something about those lunches—about Bubba's—helped Father shed the*

business persona and just be Dad for a change. He became almost human, asking us about school, girls, and even sometimes about work, but mostly just about us. Not just surface questions, mind you, but a special brand of must-know, burning-desire inquiries that made us want to spill our guts. And so we did.

He shared stories about his own life, making it a point to look deep into our eyes, a tactic I learned well and one that has contributed to much of my success, I believe. At the time I felt as though he were staring into my soul; Brendan said he felt the same way.

One of those days sticks out in my mind as if it were yesterday. Father had just asked the big question. He asked me who I wanted to be when I finished college.

Who. Not what. A million times Father and I had discussed what I wanted to be when I graduated. But that day the question was about who I wanted to become.

Was there a difference? And if so, did I have an answer?

For some reason I took offense to the question. I still don't know why it bothered me so. Maybe the ice-cold malt had frozen my brain, but instead of shooting back an intelligent answer that would make Father proud, I blurted out, "Do you even know what true success looks like?"

Brendan half laughed, half choked on his milk-shake. Father's mouth dropped open. Looking back, I realize my question sounded disrespectful, though I didn't mean it that way at the time.

Disrespect my dad? No way. In my reverent view of him, Father was the picture of success. If I turned out to be half the businessperson he was, earned half of his income, and had half of his power, I'd count that a massive success. As an interesting aside, I had to double him on all of those counts before I figured out that something was still missing. I still hadn't found true success.

Ouch. Brendan looked into the fire. Why hadn't Taylor ever said anything about feeling as though something was missing from his life? If only Taylor had really listened to Brendan in those early years, he'd have heard the answer. If only he'd listened. Brendan shook his head. He sure had tried to get through to Taylor in those days.

There wasn't a single doubt in Brendan's mind what had been missing from Taylor's life, why his success had felt empty. But in those days, Taylor wouldn't hear of God. He thought religion and all matters of faith were for the weak. He showed no signs of weakness. Ever.

Father answered my question, all right. In fact I've often wished I could forget that entire conversation ever happened. Brendan remembered it too. He's reminded me of that conversation more than once.

Father looked me square in the eyes and said, "Son, that's both complex and simple at the same time. Look—just remember this. God has given us some pretty basic commands. If you keep them, you'll find out all you need to know about success."

I asked him if he was referring to the Ten Commandments. He responded by telling me that yes, technically it was the Ten Commandments, but since I was a college boy and was accustomed to the abbreviated version of things, he could give me just two commandments that summed up all ten.

Wow, ten for the price of two? Just like David Taylor Bellows to get a deal, even on commandments from God. Thankfully there were only two to remember, because I'd long forgotten the other eight.

"Love God with all your heart and mind, and love your neighbor as you love yourself."

Um...OK. I nodded along with Dad like I understood some profound truth. Love God, and love people. How about work hard, love money, and look out for yourself? After all no one else was going to.

I faked it through the rest of the conversation. It terrified me that Father might be going soft on me. What would I do if he turned into a pandering, emotional mess like most of the religious nuts I knew? Like Brendan, whom I loved, but whom I believed never would see true success.

Brendan tried to talk to me about Father's words for at least a week after the commandment comment. I felt strangely comforted when he told me it was actually Jesus who summarized the ten into the most important two—not my dad. At least Father wasn't completely to blame.

I didn't know what my father had meant, and I didn't want to. But Brendan sure tried to open my eyes in the days following that conversation. Boy, did he ever. I think a part of me knew that once I encountered the truth I would be accountable for it.

*As someone who answers to no one but my father,
I would have no part of that.*

*Once he encountered the truth, he'd be accountable
for it?* Brendan thought, as he clasped his hands behind
his head and slouched down in his chair. Taylor sure had
nailed it. Trouble was, even by that time in his life, Taylor
already had encountered the truth too many times to count.
He was accountable for it, like it or not. Brendan blew the
air from his lungs.

Those days felt like yesterday. Could they really have
been almost three decades ago? Brendan had felt such an
urgency to get Taylor to understand what his father had
meant. That urgency never had faded through the years,
but the opportunity had.

Brendan's body jerked upright. Now that he thought
about it, it seemed odd that Taylor's dad had even said
such things. He never again gave any indication of faith
like that—at least not that Brendan knew about. It was one
moment of insight into Mr. Bellows's soul, a glimpse of
the state of his heart.

What would've happened if Taylor's father had been
more open with his son? If Mr. Bellows had raised Taylor
to know God as he, himself, apparently did? Then again
Taylor never had listened to Brendan either. It had been
the one point of contention in their friendship.

There was the time when they were little boys, probably
nine or ten years old, running along the creek bed, when
Brendan looked up at the sky and said, "Stop, Taylor. Do
you feel that?"

Taylor shook his head. "Feel what?" His gaze darted
down the creek; he seemed annoyed at the diversion.

"Just lift your face, and close your eyes. Let the sun warm your face." Brendan scrunched his eyes closed.

Taylor chuckled. "Dude, none of your sissy stuff, OK?"

"That heat?" Brendan pretended not to hear Taylor's dig. "That heat is how I know God is real." Brendan chuckled as he remembered taking off down the creek, fully expecting Taylor to follow him and knowing Taylor never would ask for an explanation—which of course he didn't.

True success? Brendan shook his head. Most of his life felt like a success to him—maybe not Taylor's definition of success…but success nonetheless.

I always will be thankful for Brendan and the way he has been there for me, even when I was being a little thickheaded. As I look back on this, it's apparent now that when I focused my life on these two simple commandments—at least in some way—things went very well for me. I understood true success.

Brendan and Allison had it right. I got away from what I knew from the beginning. I was lured into believing that success was about money, power, fame, and pleasure. If those things defined success, I should have opted for failure. My true success in life came when my focus was on doing what God wanted me to do and investing in the lives of others. My only regret is that I wasted so many years chasing the wind when I should have been all in from the start.

Chasing the wind? Brendan put the diary down and took a sip of his coffee as he reflected on the day when he had made that statement to Taylor. He had no idea how big an impact his words had made or that Taylor even had remembered what he'd said.

The campus had buzzed with activity as students packed up their rooms and prepared to head for home—or to some far-flung, real-life situation like a job. Taylor and Brendan were hanging out at the Bean Factory on the day before finals. They were going to miss hanging out there; it was the place to be on campus and where Brendan had learned the difference between good coffee and bad—a skill he'd carried with him throughout his life. It wasn't the five-dollar-a-cup trendy coffeehouse coffee that had to be doctored with syrups and fancy foam. Just coffee.

On this particular day, Allison was serving and making her usual easy conversation with the customers. Brendan sighed at the memory of Alli, as the regulars called her. The tall, slender blonde with the contagious smile and warm heart. Allison had a kind word for anyone who crossed her path. She still did actually.

"Hey, Brendan. Hey, Taylor." Allison grinned, and waved the white towel she carried. "Two cups?"

Their verbal response was in perfect unison. "Yep." But Brendan was sure he was the only one who felt the flip-flop of his stomach at her nearness—not that Allison had any idea. Finals tomorrow. Graduation three days later. Would she ever know how he felt? Or would they part ways with Alli never realizing what Brendan knew to be true? Allison was meant to be his wife.

As Brendan and Taylor settled into their favorite chairs next to the front window, Alli carried over two steaming mugs; the house-blend aroma was unmistakable.

"Ready for graduation?" Allison set a dish of creamers and some sugar on the table.

Brendan looked over the top of his cup with raised eyebrows. "Depends." *On you.*

Taylor took his first sip, placed his cup on the small round table, and looked into Allison's blue eyes. "Graduation can't come soon enough for me. How about you?"

How it was that Taylor never saw Allison the way Brendan did was either divine providence or pure luck. Brendan would take it, either way.

"I'll be glad when it's over. Some of my classes were super boring, and I'm just glad to be done with it all." Allison looked around the coffee shop. "It's been a lot of work."

"Hey, when are you through here? Want to join us so we can catch up?" Taylor tipped his head toward the side door.

Allison's eyes lit up. "Perfect timing. I just poured my last cup." She slipped her slim arms around her waist and tugged at her apron strings. "I'll clock out then meet you guys on The Deck."

Brendan and Taylor picked up their cups and sauntered out to the wide wooden deck the students used as a hangout. Sheltered by trees strung with twinkling Italian lights on all sides, it was private at night and shielded from the sun during the day. The Deck was the best place on campus to find the cool evening breeze that made for a romantic environment—perfect for drinking coffee with your favorite girl.

They chose a cherry-stained picnic table from those that lined the edge near the railing, where the lighting was best and a cool breeze always blew. Brendan lifted a leg over the bench and ducked his head to miss the string of paper lanterns strung between two light poles. To say that Allison was Brendan's favorite girl would be an understatement, only Taylor had no idea—though how he could have missed the cues was beyond Brendan. Besides, Brendan never had found the courage to ask her out for anything other than coffee, so it wasn't like he could stake some claim on her.

Brendan had heard from a mutual friend that she was interested in him, but even with that opening, he had yet to do anything about it. Now school was ending, and it seemed he might never get up the nerve. If only he were like Taylor, who was never without a date, or a girlfriend, or a companion of some kind.

After a few minutes, Allison appeared minus her green Bean Factory apron. Her hair had been freed from the band that had held it back, and now it cascaded across her shoulders.

Both men stood as she walked up. "Hey, Alli." *Please don't blush,* Brendan begged his body.

Allison set down her mug and side-saddled the bench beside Brendan. She let out a deep sigh, and Brendan opened his mouth. *Act casual*, he told himself. "So how did your classes finish up?"

"Well, with the exception of one horrible business class, pretty well. All A's if I nail my finals."

Brendan beamed. Those were hard-won grades earned through hours of late-night study after long hours serving coffee.

"What happened in your business class?" Taylor stared into his mug with disinterest.

Wait a second. Was that actual disinterest? Or was Taylor pretending like he always did when he wanted a girl to work for his attention? Brendan shook his head to clear his thoughts. Taylor wasn't interested in Allison. No way. She was a solid Christian, and he…well…wasn't. Taylor never had much use for the *good* girls. He said they put too many unnatural limits on his masculinity.

Allison shrugged, her blonde hair waving in the breeze. "I wrote a paper early this semester about my definition of success, and well…it seemed the prof and I didn't see eye to eye. He gave me a B. My only B in four years actually."

Brendan leaned forward. "OK, I've got to hear this. What did you write about?"

Alli grimaced. "That's just it. I wrote from my heart and my personal beliefs and passion. I believe that success isn't determined by dollars, power, or the bottom line. Instead I believe success is found in the lives of those we come in contact with and how we impact their lives." She shrugged. "I guess Professor Standish didn't quite appreciate the personal approach."

Brendan raised an eyebrow at Taylor. Had Allison been reading their minds? After all it had only been a week earlier that Mr. Bellows had given them his definition of success. Allison's sounded eerily similar and very much like Brendan's own. Was God trying to tell him something? Was Allison God's handpicked woman for him? Brendan sure hoped so.

Taylor shook his head. "What do you mean by that?"

Allison flung her legs over the bench and placed her elbows on the picnic table. "Well, you see, I believe God has put each of us here for a reason. Part of that reason is so he can love us and we can love him." Taylor was locked on Allison's sparkling blue eyes. No worries there; the more Allison talked, the more Taylor would be turned off. Brendan could be sure about that.

"So what's the other part of the reason?" Brendan asked. He'd say anything to keep her talking.

"I'm glad you asked." Allison grinned. "I believe the balance of our purpose is to be used by God, in his work, which is to reach others in his name. My paper went into great detail about how you should invest in God's work, and he would bless you in yours because you'd be sharing in purpose with him."

Brendan nodded. "Exactly."

Allison shot him a look of surprise. Her lips parted as though ready to ask a question.

Taylor lifted his palm. "Hold up. Hold up." He shook his head side to side. "This is a little uncanny. My father just said something very much like what you're telling us. Right, Brendan? You were there."

Brendan nodded. *Best not to speak*, he thought. *Let Taylor reveal his true heart to Allison.*

"But it sounds like I need to be in the ministry full time to do this work." Taylor sighed. "Where's the business mind in that?"

Brendan shook his head. "Not at all. Everyone can be used by God to serve him and others. In whatever role they've been called to live, whether as a high-powered exec or…" He gestured across the deck space. "…serving coffee to college students."

Allison grinned and nodded. "Precisely. We are each given a unique gift when we turn to God. The natural talents he has given each of us become part of our empowerment to do his work."

Taylor's eyebrows knitted together, as though he were trying to piece the thought into some kind of cohesive plan. The trouble was that God's business plan didn't always work the same way corporate America's business plan worked.

"So how did you conclude your paper?" Brendan leaned forward. If only he felt confident enough to reach out and grab Allison's hand. But if he could do that, he'd be Taylor.

Allison's response had the passion of a state senator trying to get a bill passed on the senate floor. "My conclusion was simple, if I invest in *God's* work, he will bless *my* work, because they are one. At the end of the day, success is doing God's will and seeing the results in the lives of those I come in contact with. Investing in the individual creates strong teams. Strong teams create strong companies. Strong companies produce the results that Wall Street desires. So, you see, serving God nets you the results the world seeks, as a byproduct of doing God's will."

There was no way Taylor ever would have heard that from Brendan. He would have scoffed and rolled his eyes if Brendan had said such a thing. But coming from Allison? Hard to say. Her business teacher had mostly rejected the concept, so Taylor had support if he chose to ridicule Allison's ideas. On the other hand, it was really difficult to argue with her logic—for a believer anyway. The whole thing had to start from a place of belief.

Taylor's eyes widened as he considered Allison's words. To Brendan it felt like waiting for a jury to return with a verdict of crazy or credible. That was the question.

Brendan closed his eyes. *Lord, please get through to him.*

Taylor blinked a few times, and the corners of his mouth turned up in a slight smile. He leaned over close to Allison. "Would you go to dinner with me?"

What? Brendan thought his coffee might make a reappearance. How could Taylor turn this conversation into a pick-up line? And why her? Why Allison? With all the other girls he'd dated and the vast array of beautiful girls who would line up to date him? Why her? Why then?

Fake it 'til you make it. Brendan pasted a smile on his face, hoping he didn't resemble an eight-year-old on Christmas when Aunt Edna gifted a box of socks and underwear. Could he forgive Taylor for swooping in on Allison? Then again he'd never told Taylor how he felt about her, so what did he expect?

Maybe she'd say no. Brendan searched Allison's blue eyes. *Please say no.*

The corners of her mouth turned up, and she flashed her pearly-white teeth. The sparkle in her eyes told Brendan all he needed to know. Allison would not be his. She'd go out with Taylor, and then he'd dump her when he got tired of her. But it would be too late for Brendan. He was out of luck.

Taylor and Allison made their plans for the evening, and Brendan did all he could to keep from sulking. On the way out of the Bean Factory, he couldn't hold it in any longer. "I just don't get it. What do you want with Allison?" He shook his head. "She's so not your type."

Taylor shrugged. "I don't really know. I haven't decided what to do with her. On one hand, I can show her what true success really is, if you know what I mean." He wiggled his eyebrows up and down.

Brendan searched the curbside. Where was the nearest trashcan in case he puked?

"On the other hand, maybe she's on to something. You know?"

"Yeah, I do know." But it stunk, just like all of Taylor's other escapades. Successful for him, painful for everyone else. "Just don't hurt her, man. She's one of the good ones." If he broke her heart…

"Yeah, maybe that's it. Even though I don't deserve it, maybe I know I need one of the good ones in my life."

"That's the thing about true success, T. It's rarely deserved."

Chapter Four
TRUE MENTORSHIP

A ringing cell phone interrupted Brendan's thoughts and brought him back from his daydreams of the past. Ah, Ann. He touched the screen. "Hello, there."

"Just checking in to see how you're doing." She was always looking out for him. Why had God blessed him with such a wonderful partner?

"Things here are OK. The coffee's hot, and the breeze is cool. Couldn't ask for more." Brendan reached beside him for the empty soda can and spat into the opening. He smiled. If Ann were there, she'd surely shudder in disgust at Brendan's snuff habit. Even he had to admit it was disgusting, but it calmed him.

He remembered the time when Ann had thought she'd grabbed her fresh can of Diet Dr. Pepper and taken a big swig. Brendan grinned at the memory of Ann's dark waves bouncing as she jumped up and down, sputtering and rubbing her tongue with the sleeve of her tennis jacket. She wasn't very supportive of his nasty habit for a long time after that.

"Great. I'll be out tomorrow afternoon in time for lunch. There are some steaks in the freezer. Can you lay them out to thaw tonight, and we can grill out for lunch tomorrow?"

That's my girl. Always thinking. "Sounds like a wonderful plan. See you tomorrow. Love you."

"Love you too."

Hmm. Dinner? What would he'd do about that? Maybe there was a pizza in the freezer.

Brendan shuffled to the kitchen and stuck his mug in the microwave, then turned to the old chest freezer on the screened-in porch just outside the back door. He rifled through the paper-wrapped packages of meats and fish. Many—probably most of them—were from hunting and fishing trips he and Taylor had taken over the years.

Brendan wondered what would happen to the full-time, four-person crew Taylor kept employed to tend to *The Treasure Chest*. He shook his head. Taylor had spent a fortune keeping a forty-foot rig ready to go at a moment's notice. A quick run down the coast. Deep-sea fishing. A little float, as he called it, across the harbor for dinner.

Come to think of it, how many employees had lost their jobs after Taylor had lost his life? The pilot and crew of his G5 jet. His assistant. His personal trainer. Allison would keep the household staff. And the company would keep going, at least unless the board of directors did something drastic. There was so much to think about, so many people affected.

There. Brendan's hands closed around two steak-size packages marked "Filets." A perfect lunch with his beautiful bride. Maybe it would be warm enough outside to sit on the deck and look out over the water at the changing leaves.

Brendan's stomach growled. When was the last time he'd eaten? A bite here, a bite there. News of Taylor's death immediately had zapped his appetite, and it hadn't returned in the ensuing days. Maybe Ann would bring it with her.

He retrieved his coffee from the microwave and returned to his spot by the fire. He lifted the journal and turned the page. " 'Two is better than one.' " *Hmm. This ought to be interesting.*

This may sound a little cliché, but true mentorship is a life lesson I didn't fully understand until midway through my career. I discovered, during a very low time in my life, that I could not do everything myself. I was under the false impression that, because of my stature in business, I was invincible and could handle any curveball thrown at me. I was wrong in a big way. I cannot imagine where I would be today if it were not for Brendan and his rock-solid faith in me, even when I was heading down the wrong road, as I did from time to time.

After Father passed away, Brendan truly became my mentor on so many levels, but more than that, he always has been my brother.

Hold it. Brendan put the book in his lap. *I was his mentor?* He pressed the tips of his fingers into his temples to relieve his headache. None of this made sense. Did Taylor actually write these journals, or was someone playing a sick joke on him?

Brendan always had positioned himself ready to be a mentor to Taylor but never had believed Taylor accepted him in that role. The teasing, the digs at Brendan's bank account, the offers of executive-level positions in Taylor's company…

He'd assumed Taylor looked down on him in some ways. That was OK. It wasn't like he needed Taylor to validate his identity. That never had been a problem. But to believe Taylor saw him as his mentor? Hard to swallow. And what was this low time in his life that Taylor was talking about? Maybe it was during the affair. Well, there was one way to find out.

Financially, spiritually, emotionally, and mentally, Brendan covered all the bases. Once, when I tried to thank him for always being there with the gift of a fine watch, he just looked at me and told me to keep it. Instead of a watch for himself, all he wanted for me to do was to find someone I could mentor—you know, invest in someone else.

Well, I was petrified because I knew how messed up I really was inside. I needed a mentor, definitely, but the responsibility of sharing my knowledge and expertise with someone else was an overwhelming weight on my shoulders. But it made sense even then. There's always someone a step behind on the journey. There's always someone who needs to be pulled along to the next stage of life. But I had no idea where to start.

*So, with Brendan's help, I began to mentor oth-
ers, though I didn't know that was what I was doing
at first. First it was young business hopefuls who
looked up to me for money or corporate expertise.
Then it was a few newly married young men, until it
became quite clear that I had no business mentoring
someone on the topic of being a good husband—but
that's a subject for another day. And then lately
I've been mentoring businessmen on how to blend
their work lives with their family lives and their
faith lives.*

Brendan scrunched his eyebrows together. "Honestly,
T," he whispered, "you might have been better off sticking
with the marriage mentorship than the faith stuff, dude."
He reached the table for his coffee mug and lifted it to his
lips. He took a small sip of the icy brew. It would need
reheating. He set it back on the table. It could wait.

All of this didn't add up. How was it that Brendan had
such a different opinion of his best friend than Taylor had
of himself? Had he missed something? He laid his head
back against the headrest and closed his eyes, the heat from
the fire warming his cheeks.

Sure, Taylor had always had people around him—
including younger, less experienced newlyweds—but
Brendan never had considered that Taylor had done it
intentionally for the purpose of mentorship. But then again,
why not? God certainly never had a habit of calling the
perfect to do his work. Instead he seemed to prefer to equip
the called once they answered.

Never one to enjoy a spoiler, Brendan was still tempted
to let his fingers travel to the back of the book to see how
it ended. Dread and excitement mingled as he considered

that the ending might be far different than he'd expected, than he'd thought he'd known.

No greater reward is there than to have, and be, a friend and a mentor. Yes, two is better than one, and Brendan has been my difference maker. I remember once when I was on my high horse celebrating my accomplishments, and he recommended I read about a true king, King David.

King David had thirty or more mighty warriors. They fought with him and for him. They were loyal. But three stood out above the rest—kind of like advisors. Right-hand guys. The ones on whom David depended to hold him up in battle, physically and spiritually.

Jesus had a similar thing going on. He had his twelve disciples, but there were three that he called out and drew closer to himself. They were beloved above the rest.

Brendan—he has been my best friend, my brother, my difference maker. But like David and like Jesus, I decided I needed three guys who would really hold me accountable in different areas of my life—different than Brendan would because we were so close.

Having those guys—Sam, Doug, and Andy, to be exact—friends of mine and Brendan's, to serve as a kind of board of directors over my life, to provide wise counsel for tough decisions, strong shoulders for hard times, and rock-solid accountability, has been a crucial part of my growth.

When we face tough decisions, we need trustworthy advice. Because when we stumble, and we

*will, we need someone to pick us up. And in our
daily lives, we need someone we can trust to hold
us accountable as we grow, which I hope I never
stop doing.*

Brendan smiled. Sam, Doug, Andy. What great guys.
So different from one another, yet somehow part of one
whole that filled a need in Taylor's life—in Brendan's life
too, really, just in a different way. He'd never been jealous
of their connection with Taylor; in fact he'd often prayed
for their wisdom as they walked with Taylor through some
of his difficult times. Those guys could call it like it was
because Taylor had given them that right. But Brendan?
Well, he had to be more careful. There was more to lose
in some ways—like when a parent must be careful with
a teenager. Sam, Andy, and Doug didn't have to worry
about that.

Brendan glanced at his watch, the one Taylor had given
to him twice—once as the thank-you gift Brendan had
turned down, then later as a different sort of gift, which
he'd accepted. It always had felt like an Ebenezer to him,
a token to commemorate the day Taylor had handed the
reins to God, the day he had left the past behind.

Sixteen years after Taylor had taken over as CEO
of Bellows Corporation, the wheels began to shake. It
seemed that nothing went right. The stock was down, and
his management team couldn't agree on a single issue. To
make matters worse, Allison was ready to leave him for a
list of reasons—all things they could work through if they
tried. It seemed that all the power and influence Taylor
possessed couldn't keep a lock on his team or his family,
and he lost his focus.

Brendan had spent hours and hours counseling Taylor. He reached out to Allison; he sent notes and made suggestions. He mentored them through the dark days of their marriage. Those days seemed the darkest possible, but time would reveal they weren't even close to the bottom of the pit. Ann, always eager to stay out of other people's business, even got involved. What had she said? "I can't sit by and watch my best friends throw away God's greatest gift to them. There's something I can do about it, and I'm going to do it."

Then, while working on a large takeover deal involving a smaller company, Taylor met Brittany Harper. The young and talented partner at Harper-Kline Incorporated immediately caught Taylor's eye during negotiations for the takeover. How had Taylor described her? "Strikingly beautiful, brunette, and athletic. Very different from Allison." Brendan knew right then that there would be trouble. He warned Taylor he was entering dangerous territory, but Taylor assured him that everything was strictly professional between him and Brittany.

But then Brendan got a chance to meet Brittany at a benefit he attended with Ann. Taylor was to be there too, but Brendan had been so surprised to find out that Allison wasn't going to be with him. They usually did things like that as a foursome. Taylor, however, was flying solo that night. At least that's what Brendan thought…until he arrived at the benefit.

Brendan entered the ballroom with the always elegant Ann floating beside him. Taylor spotted their entrance from across the room and rushed their way, but not before he motioned for an attractive woman in a royal-blue sequined gown to join him.

Several yards away, near the dance floor, the beauty lifted a very toned arm and flipped her luxurious brown waves over her tanned shoulder. *Oh, boy.* Brendan knew immediately that the woman was Brittany, and she was trouble.

"There she is." Taylor reached out an arm and pulled Brittany into the group. "I want you all to meet Brittany Harper. I've gotten to know her in the weeks since the merger talks started, and I must say I wish we could have begun a working relationship long ago."

Brittany looked up at Taylor and fluttered her eyelashes. "I'm not so sure that would've been a good idea." She gave a demure grin and flashed her brilliant teeth. The tortoiseshell frames she wore enhanced her bright-green eyes and lent her an authority despite her beauty.

Taylor might as well have been a preening peacock for all his strutting.

Was it obvious to anyone besides Brendan? A quick glance at Ann convinced him she saw it too.

Ann slid her hand down Brendan's forearm and squeezed his hand. She leaned close to his ear and whispered, "It's going to be OK, love."

But what could he do? How could he convince Taylor he was playing with fire? What if he'd already...um... played with it? He'd have to have a talk with him—not that Taylor would listen.

Brendan shook his head. As he looked back, he realized that was the problem. It was why he was having so much trouble with the mentor relationship he and Taylor supposedly had. Taylor certainly had never let on that Brendan had ever gotten through to him about most things.

Over the coming weeks following that party, Taylor had scheduled meetings late into the evenings with Brittany.

Some of them may have been necessary, but no way were they all vital to the deal those two were striking—well, the business deal anyway. It didn't take long for Taylor to begin canceling plans with Brendan, sometimes leaving Allison to attend dates and functions with Brendan and Ann alone.

Taylor had walked right into vulnerability in the pursuit of power and had fallen captive to the temptations of that beautiful woman who was accustomed to getting what she wanted. Now what?

Was Brittany innocent? No, not at all. She made no secret of her attraction to Taylor and, Brendan learned from Ann, privately bragged to her girlfriends of her quest to land the "Big One." Brendan guessed Taylor was that "Big One"—he had wealth, power, and even fame to some degree.

One afternoon Brendan sat at his desk in his downtown Manhattan office, high in the glass tower where he worked as a consultant to the Bellows Corporation. A big meeting had just taken place in the large conference room down the hall. As he was trying to sort out his thoughts, his intercom rang. "Mr. Austin."

"Yes?"

"Mr. Bellows would like to come down to see you. Do you have time for him?"

Brendan smiled at the politeness of his assistant. Asking if he "had time" for Taylor was the same as asking if he had time to take his next breath. "Yes, that will be fine. Please send him down."

What could Taylor want? Brendan stood and moved to the picture windows near his conference area. He stood two feet from the glass, staring out the floor-to-ceiling windows, taking in the view. Thankful for a clear day, he gazed north from Midtown toward Central Park, and then west toward Rockefeller Center. Intoxicating.

A gentle knock sounded at the door. Without turning Brendan simply said, "Thank you, Ms. Franklin. Please send him in."

"I'm already in. Can I sit down?"

Brendan snapped from his reverie and spun around. "Oh. Hey. Grab a seat, Taylor. I'll get the coffee." Some habits were too hard to break.

Taylor lowered his frame into a large casual chair in the seating area of the expansive office. As Brendan poured the coffee, Taylor began, "I believe we'll have this deal wrapped up by the end of the week."

"You want the usual in your coffee?"

"Yes, please." Taylor cleared his throat. "What are your thoughts on their latest proposal changes?"

What to say to that? Was it even a good idea to follow through with this deal? Brendan added cream and sugar to his coffee then took the seat across from Taylor. How much could he say? Their working relationship naturally imposed certain limits on their friendship, at least while they were in the office or talking business. Brendan had no idea what was safe—what was allowed—anymore.

His thoughts? Simple. *Walk away from the danger of anything that risks impropriety—even, or maybe especially, if it's already happened.* But he couldn't say that. He couldn't ask that.

"You want to tell me what's the matter?" Taylor's nostrils flared as if he were an impatient stallion. He lifted his phone and scrolled through it. A defense mechanism?

Brendan shrugged. "You came to see me. If you want my business opinion on the proposal, then fine. Here it is. I believe it's a fair deal for both parties, and we should close it." From a business standpoint, it was completely the truth.

Taylor's head dropped, and all the air in his lungs rushed out in a heavy sigh. "That's not why I'm here. I think you know that."

Well, if they were dispensing with the subterfuge... "Taylor, we've been friends a long time. I can read you like a book." Brendan shrugged. "If you want me to, I can be honest with you. But you have to want it."

"Yes, I know. That's why I'm here. I need your help." Taylor rubbed his temples, his knuckles turning white from the pressure.

OK, then. Brendan would jump right into the deep end. "Let me guess. Does it involve a woman named Brittany?"

Taylor whipped his head up and turned until he stared right into Brendan's eyes. His nod was barely perceptible—no more than a twitch—but his whispered plea was unmistakable. "Help."

Say no more. Brendan shifted into the chair beside his friend and leveled his gaze. His voice low and even, he asked, "How far has it gone?"

Shoulders slumped, Taylor croaked out his next words. "Too far. At the end of the meeting just now, she passed me this note." He reached a trembling hand into his jacket pocket and pulled out a crumpled pink card. He handed it to Brendan and gave a nod for him to read it.

T, meet me after dinner. Room 2324. —B

Brendan lifted his eyes and locked his gaze with Taylor's. "Wow."

"Yeah, and that's not all. Along with the note, she handed me this." He held up a hotel card key.

Did that mean…? Brendan had to find out if Taylor had been to her room on other occasions. And if so, how many times? He had to know what Taylor had done. "How many other times has she given you cards like this?"

The cup in Taylor's hand tremored as if an earthquake were about to begin…or maybe end. His eyes closed, and his body seemed to dissolve right in front of Brendan.

Taylor opened his eyes. A single tear ran down his cheek. "Just one."

Brendan placed his cup on the table in front of him, closed his eyes, and sat in silence while he rubbed his brow. That didn't mean Taylor had used the key last time, did it? But if he hadn't, this would be a victorious conversation, not a devastating one. He had used the key.

Father, please fill me with your wisdom and guidance to be a friend and counselor to Taylor. Help me steer him to righteousness. Help me steer him to forgiveness. Amen.

Taylor had moved to the windows and was staring out over the city. Lights twinkled as dusk descended upon Manhattan, casting an orange glow across the horizon. He tipped his head toward the view. "The city is so large it lures you into thinking you can hide from the rest of the world, and no one will know what you're doing. What a joke."

Brendan stood and walked toward the window, stopping just behind Taylor's shoulder. "No matter how big the city is, God always knows what you're doing." *Deep breath.* "I believe you're in my office for a reason."

"You could be right."

"Taylor, I know I'm right." Was this it? Was this the moment when Brendan would be able to find grace and truth and forgiveness? Or would he say something stupid and turn Taylor away from God forever?

Well, that was for God to decide. All Brendan could do was be obedient and point the way.

Taylor turned around slowly to face his friend, his cheeks showing evidence of the tears that had fallen. He reached out and grabbed Brendan's forearms. "Bren, I am so sorry. I need your help. What should I do?" His eyes looked haunted, scared.

Brendan slipped his hands around to grip Taylor's shoulders then gave him a gentle shake. "Brother, I won't sugarcoat the situation. That won't help anyone." He exhaled and closed his eyes for the briefest moment. "What you've done is wrong, and there will be consequences for your actions. That cannot be avoided. And I know this must seem like the end of the world—or you're afraid it will be, anyway—but you'll get through this, and I'll be by your side all the way."

The tears streamed down Taylor's face. He nodded. "Means a lot to me."

"I still believe in you. Always have and always will." Brendan felt the tension in Taylor's shoulders release upon his hearing the words of accountability and comfort.

"That helps, man. More than you could know."

Brendan knew the hard part was just beginning and the healing process would be long. If Taylor and Allison were willing to put in the work and get the right kind of help, they'd be able to save their marriage. It was up to them.

"But…Allison…" Taylor dissolved into a fresh round tears as he slumped into the black leather chair and dropped his head in his hands. His shoulders shook with sobs. "What have I done? She doesn't deserve this."

No, she didn't. But they'd deal with that in a moment. "Listen. The time for playing games with this is over. You need forgiveness. It's time to quit pretending you have it all together. It's time to approach the throne of grace, God's grace, with confidence that he'll meet your need and give you help." Brendan knelt in front of Taylor's chair. "That's in the book, man. It's a promise."

Taylor locked eyes with Brendan. He nodded. "It is time."

I remember the moment I accepted Jesus into my life and made him Lord over me. Until that moment I'd fought it every step of the way. I had denied my need because I thought turning to God made me weak and vulnerable, and I wanted to be neither of those things. I thought I would be stronger if I just walked my own path. But it was in my deepest moment of need, in the midst of my pain and desperate fear, that I realized how weak I truly was when I walked alone.

Brendan showed me that all the grace and forgiveness and mercy I needed was at the feet of Jesus. It was ready for me and waiting there. I just had to reach out and take it.

So I did.

Brendan, God love him, knelt right there on that floor in his dress pants—the manly man that he is, humbled and willing to kneel before his friend and his God. Oh, that I would ever be half the man Brendan is! He put his hand on my shoulder, and I felt compelled to look into his eyes. Then my friend, my brother, said those life-giving words. "Pray with me."

So I did. "Father," I repeated after Brendan. "I'm a stubborn man and a selfish man. I come to you broken and humbled. Please forgive me for the sins of unbelief and pride. Please forgive me for walking through my life apart from you. Draw me to your side, and wash me with your grace and mercy."

Then Brendan said the coolest thing. And I believe it was a prayer I've seen God answer. Brendan prayed, and I repeated, "Please birth passion in me to share you with others."

Having taken on a new life in that moment of my sorrow, I had hope and promise. I hoped Allison would forgive me, but I knew for sure God had. There was hope for my marriage and assurance of eternal life. And suddenly I had a new reason to be a mentor. But first I had to wade through the mess I'd created.

Wow. Brendan remembered the day like it with yesterday. What a privilege it had been to lead his best friend to Christ. Walking with Taylor into his home a little while later and listening to him tell Allison what had happened was one of the hardest things he'd ever had to do. But his friend had needed him. Taylor couldn't break his wife's heart alone.

Brendan had stayed long enough to comfort Allison, give strength to Taylor, and then assure them both that Taylor was a changed man. The tears continued long after he left—Brendan was sure—but God had it all under control. Even amid those dire circumstances, God's grace had shone so brightly.

Strangely Brendan never had realized that he had acted as a mentor to Taylor in that situation—and now that he thought about it, in many other ways too. Maybe it was just because he was being guided by God and doing what he knew was right that it didn't feel like he had a title like "mentor." But that's what he'd been. Maybe he should be more intentional about it in the future. After all, two really are better than one.

Chapter Five
TRUE LEADERSHIP

Lights flickered in the driveway then flooded the room through the picture window. Who was it? Brendan squinted against the glare and made out the shape and silver glint of Ann's SUV. She had come early! Oh, how she knew him.

He placed the diary down, stood, and rushed to the front door. The screen door creaked as he pushed it open. A gust of wind caught it just right and ripped it from his grip. It banged against the wall, and the upper hinge tore from the frame. There'd be time enough to worry about it in the morning. Nothing could bring him down in this moment.

Ann jogged through the wind to the bottom step of the wide porch, where Brendan stood reaching out to her. She wrapped her arms around his neck and buried her face in his sweater. No words were needed.

Standing there in the glow of the moonlight, Brendan and Ann held each other close—one needing comfort, the other needing to give it. Each breath brought their heartbeats closer in sync until they became one.

Brendan felt the confusion ease from his mind. The tension oozed from his shoulders and neck. The anger... Wait. Anger? Had he been angry? If so, why? He would have to explore that later. But not now...

He pulled back his head and waited for Ann to follow. She gazed up at him, wisdom and love reflecting from the brown and gold glints in her eyes. Brendan lowered his head and kissed his wife's soft lips. The final notes of strain disintegrated.

The moment could have gone on for hours, and Brendan wouldn't have minded. Taking his wife by the arms, he gently held her back far enough to look into her eyes. In a whisper, he spoke the first words of the evening. "I love you. Thank you for coming up early."

Ann fought back the tears that were being forced to the surface from the emotion of the tender moment. She rested her head on Brendan's chest and in a muffled voice replied, "I love you too, sweetie. I just couldn't stay away. Not now. You needed me."

Holding each other close, they walked, arms locked, into the cabin.

***

The morning sun peeked through the windows, casting a ray of brilliant light across Brendan's pillow. Rolling over, he squinted in the bright morning light.

"Amen." Ann forked a bite of eggs into her mouth. Brendan went right for the biscuits and gravy. They ate in silence for a few moments until Ann cleared her throat.

Uh-oh. Brendan clenched. *Here it comes.*

"So you've been digging into that diary for many hours now. What are you finding?" Ann chewed slowly while she waited for Brendan's reply.

"I must admit that it's more than I expected. Taylor's diary has been quite the read. Although the memories are somewhat overwhelming, I seem to be getting through all right."

Ann's face glowed from the sunlight that streamed through the windows behind her. Peering over the top of her cup, she asked, "What did he write about?"

"Well, there are multiple volumes that each seem to span an entire year. I started with *The Summary*, the final volume. Between the childhood memories, and the college years, and Taylor's marital struggles, I feel like I've relived everything we went through together." Brendan let out a huge sigh. "And then some."

Ann's eyebrows knitted together in confusion. "What do you mean by 'and then some'? That's the part I'm curious about."

Brendan nodded. "It's just that Taylor—I don't know—hid some of himself from me. Either that, or I was so clueless I didn't see the truth. I watched him to change his behavior, but I didn't allow him to fully change my perception of him. I never really let my opinion of him catch up to God's opinion of him." He shook his head. "Whatever the case, it's messed up."

Ann patted Brendan's hand. "I'm sure it's not as bad as that. You were a good friend to him and a great leader."

Brendan shrugged. "I don't know anymore. A good leader would have seen the growth and the potential and really nurtured it. Besides, Taylor was the leader."

"No." Ann shook her head vehemently. "You're missing the point of what a true leader is. Bren, a leader isn't just the guy at the top of the totem pole. It's not the guy who's the most successful. Not the one who gets paid the most or has the best results at changing other people."

"Keep talking." Brendan locked eyes with Ann's. Maybe she could make sense of this.

"What kind of leader was Jesus? Was he the boss? Was he the head honcho in charge of everyone?" She shook her head. "No. He was the servant of all. Humble."

Brendan nodded. She was right. Now how would he apply it to this situation?

"You need to go keep reading. That's what we're here for. And I believe it'll all come together for you. God is faithful like that, you know?"

Brendan nodded. "Yes. He is."

"Just do me one favor, OK?" Ann's eyebrows rose.

He squeezed her hand. "Anything for you, love."

"Promise me that, as you read, you'll keep in mind that a leader stirs other people to greater things. That's true. But *greater things* are different in God's eyes than they are to the world. A true leader helps others find true success—God's success."

Ann reached her hand up and tipped Brendan's chin until he was looking into her eyes. "True leaders serve other people as they point them toward Jesus. You may not have had a hand in Taylor's business success, but you guided him to the savior, Jesus Christ, with your words and your actions."

"That's all very true. And it definitely helps—trust me. But I'm finding that Taylor pursued growth in truths I had no part in teaching him." Brendan shrugged. "It's just a bit hard for me to take. But I'll get over it, because the end result was always the goal."

Ann shook her head. "No, no, no. I don't buy that for a minute. God orchestrated every step of Taylor's spiritual journey, even though Taylor didn't check with you every step of the way. He worked through you, Brendan, either by things you said or by the example you lived. You know, it's not about *you* teaching Taylor step by step. It was always about God reaching out to him through you. You were a vessel, and in freeing yourself to be that vessel, you allowed God to make a difference."

Brendan let the words wash over him. So true. So freeing. This wasn't about him at all. It was about God doing his kingdom work through Brendan in the life of Taylor, and then through Taylor into the lives of those he mentored. It really was a picture of true leadership.

Ann smiled softly. "Now go read."

Brendan grabbed a fresh cup of coffee and headed for his chair. Along the way he picked up Taylor's diary from the fireplace mantle and tucked it under his arm. Scrunching deep into the chair, he paused for a moment to take in the spectacular morning view. The sun glinted off the water. Birds flew low in search of their breakfast. Leaves fell as winter approached. Breathtaking.

After a long sip, Brendan placed his cup on the side table, reclined deeper, and opened the journal to where he'd left off.

He turned the page to the next entry, "True Leadership."

Funny how God works. Brendan smiled to himself as he imagined how many times over the years God had answered his questions before he'd even asked them. Today was no different. God had brought the topic of leadership to his heart in the minutes before he would read Taylor's words on that very subject.

Brendan closed his eyes and allowed the warmth he felt to fill his heart. He was so loved…by God and by his wife. He was ministered to even before he knew his own need. He wasn't alone in this journey. He could get through this.

So what was he waiting for?

I have learned over the years that "leadership" is a widely misused word. Once, early in my career, I believed that being a leader meant being tough while barking out orders. It was my thinking that the leader should have all the answers, and others needed to only do as the leader said and everything would be fine. With that philosophy driving me, my leadership style could only be described as "autocratic" at best.

Many times I remember calling young associates into my office for a marathon meeting only so I could hear myself talk and show them just how smart I thought I was. It was clear; this was my company, and I would run things my way. That was that. No matter the situation or the person, I made it clear I was in charge and they were there to do as I said.

My justification was simple; we made money. We made money, and we were experiencing growth in all divisions. As I looked around, it was easy for me to take credit for all that was happening. I insulated myself from the truth right before my eyes.

It was a classic case of the "emperor with no clothes." I had the people who worked for me petrified to say anything that contradicted what I said for fear of losing their jobs. Because of the wall of insecurity I had built around me, it was hard to see the true results of my leadership style. Turnover was through the roof. Our best and brightest were leaving at an alarming rate. Those who did stay could not be motivated beyond their eight-to-five positions without threats and a highly competitive workplace driven by fear of failure or job loss. So they worked long hours and stabbed their comrades in the back whenever they could. It was only a matter of time before the negative atmosphere began to provide results to match.

I would still be looking for the answers if Brendan hadn't been the one to tell the emperor he was naked. In his infinite wisdom, Bren recommended I spend some time with a friend of his from Dallas. John was the CEO of another successful company and was close to mandatory retirement age. Brendan thought it would be time well spent if the three of us went on a short fishing trip together.

It was absolutely the worst time for me to go away. Numbers had tanked the previous month. We were desperately swimming upstream to avoid a second month of negative revenues. We were about to get a quarterly valuation, and those numbers would prove crucial to our stock prices. My right-hand man had given his two-week notice and accepted an executive position with a competitor. And my marriage was barely staying afloat after my affair.

Fishing? Was Brendan crazy?

Well, in the end, I went kicking and screaming on the best trip of my life.

To me a fishing trip meant an ocean view from my forty-foot fully staffed yacht. It meant five-star meals plucked right from the ocean, and relaxing evenings under the stars. Very little effort was involved, at least on my part. I'd earned a bit of luxury, right?

But to this John guy from Dallas, a fishing trip was a far different thing.

We all met in Wyoming, probably the one state in the nation I'd yet to visit for any length of time. I quickly found out there was a reason I hadn't been there before. It's certainly not the easiest place to get to. We had to fly the G5 into the FBO in Steamboat Springs, where John met us. Then we made a two-hour drive to our drop-off point at Little Snake River. Then, much to my surprise, there was no fancy boat waiting for us there—nothing but a canoe.

A canoe? With paddles?

I mean, I was a fit guy. I worked out. I could run on the treadmill with the best of them. I loved to hike and be outside. But the thought of getting into that little canoe with two other grown men for however long it took to get to the end of that river so we could get out? I wasn't interested. In fact my only question was "Why?" Why would they even want to? We had other options, better options. And I said just as much.

"John, I appreciate your efforts, but we could have stayed in New York and enjoyed my fully

appointed yacht. In a few hours, we'd be enjoying a four-course meal under the stars."

John just listened. He didn't say a word.

"Surely you must agree that's a better plan than this." With what had to be a look of disgust, I gestured to the canoe bobbing in the river.

John said nothing.

"I mean, I've worked hard to avoid situations where I have to work this hard." I pointed at the paddles. "How will we eat? How will we sleep?" I turned in a full circle, searching for other options.

"We'll have some time at a great lodge. But then we'll head upstream, where we'll camp for a couple of nights," John said, as he smiled like a grandpa looking down at his grandson. "You don't have to worry. I've done this trip plenty of times. You're safe with me as your guide."

Safety? I turned what had to be wild eyes on Brendan. This guy thought safety was the concern? "You want us to camp outside for two nights when there's apparently a perfectly good lodge somewhere? Are you crazy?"

It was maddening how John, and even Brendan, just stood there and listened. They didn't defend themselves or explain their decisions. They just waited for my bad attitude to pass then continued with their plans.

Well, if I couldn't convince them to make other plans, I was going to take charge—whether they liked it or not. So, in fitting style for me, I barked orders at them. "Toss this in there." "Tie this down here." "Shut this off." "You paddle on the right. You paddle on the left."

And they let me. Our canoe got up the river to the lodge just fine with me in charge, even though they knew more about both canoes and rivers than I did.

Along the way we stopped to take advantage of some fast-running shallow water, which I learned was a prime spot for our target audience, the cut-throat trout. Aptly named, I thought.

As I put on my latest, top-of-the-line gear from Orvis, I felt a bit out of place. We were in God's country, and God didn't care about name-brand equipment apparently.

I walked into the swift current. The water rushing by our feet kept a steady cadence against the deafening silence. My first steps were unsure; then, once I got the hang of the new waders, I was able to maneuver around the knee-deep stream like an old pro. Not that I was proud of that accomplishment. Once I found firm footing, I threw my fly back and forth into the water around me.

"Taylor, you want to catch fish today?" John called from across the stream.

What kind of question was that? I wanted to retort, "I didn't fly halfway across the country just to stand up to my knees in water. I could have done that at home in my pool." Instead I offered a simple, "I do hope to eat tonight."

It suddenly occurred to me there were no helpers around to clean the fish. But surely that couldn't mean... Wait a second... I had to clean my own fish? Well, if that wasn't a far cry from pulling mahimahi from the Atlantic and handing it to the chef while it was still flapping and squirming, I didn't know what was.

John moved across the stream toward me, keeping his eyes locked with mine the entire time. "If you were a fish on a sunny day, where would you hide?"

If I were a fish? More Zen stuff from John. "If it were me, I would be in the shade today."

"And why would you be there?"

"To stay cool." I thought for a moment more. "And underwater visibility probably would be better from a shaded spot. I could see what was coming."

"Exactly! So wouldn't it make sense to drop your bait in the shade?"

There was logic to this thing? Who knew?

"You know, Taylor, fish are a lot like people in this regard," John said. "To understand what people are going to do, you need to know what people want." He rubbed his chin. "Who are you? That's a question I frequently ask those who work for me. The answer to that question tells you volumes about others and what drives them to do what they do. And if you're honest with your own answer, it will tell you a lot about yourself."

Brendan laid his head back and smiled. He'd often wondered what John and Taylor had been talking about over there in the sunshine that hot day—and why they hadn't moved into the shade. He wondered how many other such conversations they'd had on that trip. Knowing John, he would next expose Taylor to a lesson about yesterday's fish. At least Brendan hoped so…

So I moved into the shade and asked John if he'd ever caught a lot of fish where I now stood.

John raised one eyebrow. "Taylor, be sure you're not trying to fish yesterday's fish."

Huh? I should have known a lesson was coming, but still I asked, "Yesterday's fish? What do you mean?"

"Yesterday's successes are great, but leave them there. Learn from yesterday, and apply that knowledge to today. Use the past to create a vision for the future. But don't camp there in the past."

Hmm. "That makes a lot of sense from a business perspective."

John shook his head. "It's not just business. It's all of life. You can't fish where the fish are right now, because that moment is gone. You have to envision where they're going to be and put your fly there."

I didn't know what to make of that. I pondered John's words as I reeled in a few trout, trying not to think about the step between catching them and eating them.

Somewhere in the hours when the sun began its descent, it hit me.

At the end of the day, it wasn't about me; it was about the fish. Who are they? Where are they going? And how are they going to get there?

Brendan allowed a slow smile to spread across his face as he set the diary down and took a long sip of his coffee, newly reheated by his wife.

Warm hands squeezed his shoulders. Brendan jumped and glanced up at Ann, who stood smiling behind him. He closed his eyes and leaned back against the headrest as she kneaded the muscles in his neck.

"It's great to see you smile. What brought this on?"

"Oh, Taylor told a funny story that made me remember some really happy times. Something I'd forgotten about... something I'd never really paid much attention to, actually."

"So what was it?" She squeezed his muscles.

"It was a fly-fishing trip he and I took down the Little Snake River with John Parker from Dallas."

"I vaguely remember that. Seems like forever ago."

"Yes, it was quite a few years back. John was at the funeral. Looked healthy..." John would outlive them all, no doubt.

Ann moved to the arm of Brendan's chair and looked into his eyes. "Good trip?"

"Very. Seems Brendan got some lessons about leadership on that trip. And none of us had intended for that to be the focus. It was just supposed to be a simple getaway."

Ann's eyes twinkled. "Ah. Like I said, vessels."

That's where I learned being a leader is more than barking out orders. Boy, I sure have done my share of that, even on that trip. But, no, being a true leader is all about serving others and understanding their needs. It's about helping them reach their goals, even if they don't quite know what they are.

True leadership is only possible when a person can correctly answer three questions:

1. Who am I? For too long my identity was the head of Bellows International. The fact that I was a husband or a friend came second. And the fact that I was a born-again believer in Jesus Christ

61

came as a distant third. For too long that part of me was nothing more than an afterthought. How could I lead others with priorities like that?

2. Where am I going? My goals were defined by the bottom line. While I thought I was a business mogul with a grand vision, in reality my scope was so limited. Eventually I realized the end goal for my journey needed to bring glory to God while helping others find true potential.

3. How am I going to get there? Vision is great, but execution only happens by drawing closer to God. Through studying his word and meditating on the leading of the Holy Spirit, we see God's plans for us and how he wants us to impact others. We also need to be intentional about taking the journey with those who need us and with others whom we need.

So one day, around this time, I was doing my daily Bible reading.

Brendan glanced up from his reading to find Ann had settled on the couch across from him with a book. "Babe, he's about to quote Scripture."

"I'm not surprised." Ann smiled but didn't look up from her reading.

Here. Let me just show you what I found in John 13.

"You call me Teacher and Lord, and rightly so, for that is what I am. Now that I, your Lord and Teacher, have washed your feet, you also should wash one another's feet. I have set you an example that you should do as I have done for you. Very truly I tell you, no servant is greater than his master, nor is a messenger greater than the one who sent him. Now that you know these things, you will be blessed if you do them."

That's it. That's exactly what I had been finding—from what Allison had said those many years ago in the coffee shop, and from watching Brendan live it out every single day in front of me.

To be an effective leader, you must be a servant.

No person is greater than another. Even Jesus humbled himself to serve those who followed him. If I would do those things, I'd be blessed. And obviously so would the people I served.

It was like an epiphany. All those years of hearing similar things and encountering the concept in different ways finally came together to make sense.

Once I realized that leading meant serving, and once I really began to apply it to my leadership at Bellows, Inc., we began to see a shift in our turnover rate, and the overall morale began to change.

I am proud to write that our company has been voted as Forbes magazine's best company to work for multiple times over the last several years. This has been one of my greatest achievements in life because, of all the awards we've received, this one was voted on by our employees.

The people I serve.

Chapter Six
TRUE COURAGE

Brendan fingered the gilded edges of the journal. Three weeks had passed since he'd last opened it. Wow. He'd only intended to step away for a few days to ponder what he'd discovered from Taylor about mentorship and leadership, and even faith. Surprise, surprise. But those days went on longer than he'd planned. Life had pressed in, and it had been too difficult to dive back in; he certainly didn't want to rush through them. They deserved more finesse than that. Or maybe he just needed a break.

He looked at his watch. Taylor's gift. Three hours until the other guys arrived at DFW, and then ninety minutes for them to get up to the B2B Ranch. He might as well use the time wisely.

Another overstuffed leather chair. Another massive stone fireplace. Except this time, instead of cabin decor, wild game mounts and bearskin rugs surrounded Brendan. He was at the classic hunting lodge on the three-thousand-acre ranch he now owned.

Thank you, Taylor. He glanced around the space. *But I'd rather have you here.* Brendan opened the book. Well, in many ways, Taylor was there.

Having figured some things out sure helped in dealing with people, but I had a long way to go when it came to personal and moral decisions. Allison and I—well, it was a rocky road, and it took us a long time to get to a place where we were sure we'd stay together. She even moved out for a short time. But both of us, even in the middle of all the pain, knew we were meant to be together.

And even more it became a question of what we believed about God. Did we believe that he was able to restore us to a right relationship with him and with each other? Or did we believe the lies of our enemy, who said we were doomed? It was up to us.

We chose to believe the promises of God. And to this day, we are ever so grateful. But even while that miracle was happening, I was still screwing up.

You know, in business it's easy to convince yourself there are no black and whites. The gray areas become places of moral decay, but they're often the easiest places to be. God's calling rests far outside the gray areas in life and in business, but it took me a long time to realize that.

One time at the ranch, Brendan and I built a fire outside, and we each pulled up a chair and sat down to talk. It wasn't as if we didn't talk all day, every day. But there's something about a couple of guys sitting around a bonfire that lowers the inhibitions. So I told Brendan about what was going on at Bellows at the time. We were being pursued by a much larger company and were in a good position for a merger.

The executives at this other company dangled an insider-trading deal before me. They didn't actually call it that, but that's what it was. I was so tempted. To be a major part of a global enterprise and reap the rewards of wealth I could never imagine? How could I not chase after such a thing?

As a young businessman, I knew it was tempting but also something my father never would have considered. By the world's standards, I had to take the deal, but something held me back.

I'd been losing sleep over what once would have been a clear choice. So I brought the matter to Brendan.

Brendan looked into the fire and poked it with a stick a few times. He probably was praying over what he would say to me, knowing Bren.

I couldn't believe what he said. He told me the story of David and Goliath. I mean, I'd heard it before, as a child. But I had no idea where he was going with it because it didn't apply to business at all. But Bren had the floor.

Brendan smiled at the memory. He'd suspected the point he'd wanted to convey to Taylor that night had ever gotten through to him. Brendan had wanted to show Taylor that David wasn't unafraid as he stood before Saul and promised to save the nation of Israel. It wasn't about the absence of fear. It was about faith in the Almighty. David didn't think about what he was able to do; he was only concerned with what God was able to do.

Brendan said the following words to me. "David, a weak teenager, stood before the king and said, 'Your servant will save you.' " David knew he wasn't this mighty champion. But he knew he could stand before the giant and be victorious, not because of what he was, but because of what God was. He couldn't have had victory if he hadn't first taken that step in faith.

That's where I was that day with my company. I could live in defeat. I could react as everyone in the world would and chase the money. Or I could stand before the giant, confident I was a champion, not because of what I did, but because of what God could do.

So, in a crazy twist of events, I stood before the president of the company, who was about to swallow me whole, and I said no.

I'll never forget the look on the giant's face. He'd never been turned down before—not like that. Not by someone like me, staring untold riches right in the face and saying no. No. It was easy, really.

The powerful businessman exploded in a fit of rage. He declared my impending ruin and swore he would systematically destroy me and my company. Brick by brick.

The strange thing was, I found it funny. I knew there was nothing he could do to me that wouldn't have to pass through God's hands first. I chuckled and held the door for him as he stormed from my office with smoke billowing from his ears.

In the coming weeks and months, he remained true to his words. In his quest to destroy Bellows Corporation, however, he found himself exposed and at legal risk, due to multiple cases against him from the SEC.

The timing of this was beyond coincidence. It could have come only from God. Ultimately the deathblow to his enterprise came when he was sentenced to prison on thirty counts of fraud and embezzlement, leaving the companies he led vulnerable—exactly where I would have been had I participated. Instead Bellows Corporation came in and acquired the companies for pennies on the dollar, taking us to next level, when we became Bellows International.

Instead of acquiring Bellows in a shady deal that would leave us all susceptible to legal troubles, he unintentionally had positioned things so that Bellows Corporation had acquired his company and became Bellows International.

The weak had swallowed the giant.

Brendan flipped the journal over and laid it across his lap. He'd had no idea Taylor saw it that way. When the story of David and Goliath had come to him by the fire, he didn't really know how God would use it. And Taylor, being the private man he was, didn't report back how he had felt about the outcome of the merger.

Sure, Brendan knew what God had done with the acquisition, but he didn't realize Taylor had made the connection.

Huh. Brendan smiled. Guess he could add this to the list of times he'd been used as a mentor to Taylor. Oh, there was another time too.

A few years after this merger temptation, Taylor faced a similar challenge when he was positioned in a strategic acquisition of the company of which Brittany Harper was a partner. Brendan shook his head. It was a story he'd much rather forget. He definitely understood the business sense the merger made. Bellows International needed a stronger foothold in the fast-growing South American market, and Brittany's company was the key to corner the market.

The only problem was that, to do the deal, Brittney demanded to be placed on the board of directors, which put her in direct contact with Taylor on a regular basis. There was no way around this; if he wanted her company, he had to take her.

From a business standpoint, as with the previous trial, Taylor needed to go through with the deal, but Brendan counseled him over and over. He told Taylor he couldn't do it. Come to think of it, it was one of the few times Brendan's counsel had been that direct.

As Brendan saw it, the only way Taylor could prove his repentance to Allison and protect himself from further entanglements with Brittany was to completely end any personal and business relationship with her—which Taylor thought he'd done, until this merger opportunity arose. Taylor had to cut ties completely, or Allison would never trust him. Their marriage would be over.

So had Taylor said anything about this in his journal? Brendan flipped the book over and thumbed a few pages ahead.

Oh, I was so mad at Brendan. How dare he make such a suggestion? Like he had any idea what it would mean to the company if he canceled the merger, or for that matter, what it would mean to his marriage if he didn't. It was my business. Period.

His was one of the voices shouting in my head. Then there was the one that whispered—you know, the one that was usually harder to hear but always right. It said, "Brendan loves you; he has your very best interests at heart. Yours and Allison's. No, in this case, Bellows International takes a backseat to your spiritual well-being and the state of your marriage. Brendan is right."

So I called a meeting. I left no opportunity for comments. It wasn't open for discussion. The deal was off.

Brittany made eye contact with me for the briefest of moments as she left my office for the last time. Quickly she lowered her gaze, as though embarrassed. As the door shut, I did something I seldom did at that time in my life; I prayed for someone else.

Brendan heard the sound of a car door slamming. And then another. And another. The guys had arrived.

Laughter mingled with the clomping of boots as three of Brendan's best buddies stomped the snow from the bottoms of their feet before throwing open the big oak door.

"Hi, honey. We're home!" Andy Schumer was the first one in. Brendan smiled at the sandy-haired ex-quarterback. Just what he needed. Andy was sure to light up the weekend of work.

Sam followed, his ruddy complexion and wiry red hair a comforting sight. "Hey, bro. How's it going? You doing OK?" Leave it to Sam to get right to the point.

Brendan smiled as he gave Sam's hand a solid shake, followed by a grasp on his forearm. "I'm doing OK, man. I really am."

Lugging three packed duffels and three cases filled with the latest in archery gear, Doug stumbled through the front door. "I could sure use some help here, guys," he said. "Wouldn't want to put you out or anything."

"Well, no one asked you to bring in all our stuff." Sam strode across the room to help Doug pull in the bags.

"Yeah, well, someone had to do it." Doug unzipped his camo vest.

"Not this very instant." Andy scowled at Doug's back.

Uh-oh, Brendan thought. *Must have been a tense car ride from the airport.* "All right, all right. Simmer down, you two." Brendan pulled Doug in for a hug and clapped him on the shoulder. "Thanks for coming."

Doug looked him in the eye. "I wouldn't have missed it for the world."

Brendan lifted a hand and motioned toward the kitchen. "I've got some coffee brewing. Shall we?"

"Just what the doctor ordered." Andy rubbed his hands together.

They filed into the expansive kitchen, the place where they'd surely spend most of the weekend. Taylor used to say the whole place could fall down, but if the kitchen stood strong, people would still come. With its floor-to-vaulted-ceiling windows and the man-size stone fireplace, he was probably right. The comfortable barstools, pulled up to a huge island in the center of the room, created an inviting conversation hub, and the dining table, which faced the view on one side and the fireplace on the other, could seat fourteen people. It was definitely a place to hang out.

"So…" Sam straddled a stool at the island and warmed his hands around his mug. "Can you give us a rundown of what we're doing this weekend? I mean, besides the obvious."

Doug chose the seat next to Sam and reached into his pocket for the tiny spiral notebook he was never without. He flipped open to a new page and grab the pen from behind his ear. "OK. To-do list. Go." He waited with his pen poised over the paper.

Brendan laughed from his stance across the island. "Boy, you guys sure don't waste any time." Which was great. Architects were due out in no more than a week with hopes that construction would begin by summer. There was so much to do to get the ranch ready by then.

Where would he start? He had the guys for a little more than two days, which wasn't enough time to start any major building projects.

"This is really more of a planning session. I'm thinking we'll make a lot of notes," Brendan said, as he smiled at Doug, who was scribbling away. "We'll walk the grounds and brainstorm ways to make this a place where families will want to come year after year. Maybe we'll get a chance to map out some of the locations for the various buildings and activities. Maybe we'll mock up a calendar of sorts."

Sam nodded. "Sounds good. Your basic brainstorming session."

"With a little hunting on the side?" Andy raised an eyebrow. "It *is* hunting season, my man. All work and no play makes Andy a very dull boy."

"Well, we can't have that." Brendan shook his head. "I noticed you all brought your gear. I'm sure we'll have an opportunity to use it."

Doug nodded, all business. "Great. But if we don't get a chance to hunt, that's fine. We're here for the families who'll come here hoping for change. Right, guys?"

Brendan took a sip of his coffee. God sure had blessed him with three great friends. The five of them had made such a great team—all different yet each one-fifth of the machine. Somehow, though, it always felt like he and Taylor went a little deeper because their relationship was the only one that went back before adulthood. All the others had joined later. "Hey, can I ask you guys something?" he said.

Andy nodded. "Of course. Shoot." He straddled one of the stools at the island and propped his face on his hands.

Doug stepped around from the back. "What's up?"

"I know you guys knew Taylor thought of you as his 'Mighty Three.' You know, like David had three, and Jesus poured into three of his twelve disciples more than the others? You knew that, right?"

Sam nodded. "Yeah, he asked us to be that to him. Actually he said it was your idea."

Brendan snorted. "You know how ideas were with Taylor. You say one thing and... Well, in my case it was that he should read about King David. But Taylor read about King David then pulled out this life-changing idea and applied it to his life in a huge way that changed the world. You know?"

"Yep. That was Taylor, for sure." Andy laughed. "Yeah. The four of us went to a men's rally one time. While we were there, he asked us to fill that role in his life, in a formal sort of way. One of us with a focus on financial decisions, one of us to help him with purity of his heart and mind, and so on. He said we were like his board of directors, and you were the CEO."

"So…" How could Brendan ask this without sounding like a kid who'd been left off the baseball team? "So were you all each other's Mighty Three? How did that work?"

"No, it wasn't even as formal to us as it was to him," Sam said. "But each of us, I think, applied some of those principles in different ways to our own lives and relationships. But Taylor took it very seriously. He meant it. He wanted to keep his powerful, difference-maker relationship, which was with you, Brendan, separate from his relationship with us, his Mighty Three." Sam shrugged.

"You have to understand," Doug said, jumping in, "that Taylor functioned in life as he did in the boardroom. You can have a president of the company or an owner and a board of directors. They serve different capacities, and those duties often don't overlap for the betterment of the company. That's precisely how he saw this function of relationships in his life."

"So I guess what I'm getting at is… Well, I could use a Mighty Three in my life. You guys up for the job?" Brendan felt his cheeks pinking.

Sam nodded. "You know what? Me too, man."

Doug slapped the granite. "Look, we're four dudes who are the best of friends. Why are we beating around the bush about this thing? I mean, next we're going to pass around a note after study hall."

"Good point." Brendan laughed. "I think we need to be each other's Mighty Three. David and Jesus had it right. And so did Taylor."

"I'm in." Andy reached out a flat hand, palm down.

"Count me in." Sam laid his hand atop Andy's.

Doug grinned and added his hand to the pile. "Wouldn't miss it."

Brendan reached out two hands and gripped those of his friends. "I love you guys. We need each other."

"I think we should pray." Sam looked each man in the eyes. "Let's start this thing right...for Taylor."

"For Taylor." Brendan's eyes swam as his friends took turns praying for their new relationship. *Lord, thank you.*

"I know you guys must think I'm crazy for jumping into this a month after Taylor passed. Maybe I am, but this ranch for people and families in crisis always has been a dream of mine. I never dreamed it could be here at B2B. What a fitting legacy for Taylor." Brendan wiped away a tear from the corner of his eye.

Sam moved to the window and looked at the snowy grounds that spread out before him for acres and acres. "It *is* such a fitting legacy. There couldn't be a better place. I'm so with you, my friend."

"Yeah, me too." Doug shrugged. "I just don't think you needed to leave your position at Bellows to pull this off. You could have hired people to do the work here and then visit on the weekends to check the place out and keep an eye on things."

Sam turned from the window. "Yeah. I mean, it took a lot of courage to resign from the company. You've got a lot of life left in you to have given up such a great career."

Andy shook his head and spoke up. "No, don't you see, man? Brendan is the one. He's the guy who's going to make the difference in these families' lives. It's not just about giving them a place to go; it's about being a difference maker. Is that right, Brendan?"

Brendan nodded. "Yeah, that's it. Being a difference maker for as long as God will use me."

Doug shook his head. "I totally agree. I couldn't do it, though. I can be a difference maker on the weekends. I need to know I've got money in the bank and health insurance for my wife and me. I can't function without a retirement plan in place."

"Right." Andy jumped in. "And for me work is a place to get away from it all. Retired? At fifty? Are you sure you're ready to spend the rest of your life this way, with just you and Ann? No paycheck. No health insurance. You sure?"

It wasn't like he had to worry about money, thanks to Taylor's careful planning. "That's all great for you guys, because that's where God has called you to be. But for me?" Brendan shrugged. "You know, I watched Taylor give his heart, soul, and life to that company for thirty years. He almost lost his marriage. He did lose his life." He shook his head. "No, the courageous choice, in my opinion, isn't the one I've made. I want nothing more than to do exactly as you described, Sam. And I can't think of a better place to do it." Brendan waved his hand at the window. "This is heaven."

He strode to the window and gazed at the expanse of land. "We'll use the outdoors as a way to help people really connect with God and then with family. The ranch will be a self-sustained, multipurpose conference center, retreat destination, working ranch and farm, and fair-chase, managed hunting preserve." Brendan whipped around and grinned at his friends. "People can come for a week, a month, a summer…whatever they need, depending on where they're at. The goal is that when they leave they'll be *all in*." He lifted his hands. "Doesn't that sound amazing?"

Andy joined Brendan at the window. "It sure does, my man. And I know Taylor would agree."

"Yes! In fact I don't think you guys know something about Taylor and Bellows International. Here. Let me read you this from his journal." Brendan raced to the leather chair in the sitting room and retrieved the journal from the armrest. He flipped to a page near the end.

So there I was, raking in more dough than I could ever spend. I was working my tail off day after day, week after week, month after month, then having nothing—well, I had plenty to show for it, but no time to enjoy it. Life was swallowing me up. I felt like I existed only for the purpose of providing salaries for the hundreds of people who worked for me. Or for bringing home a paycheck for Allison. I didn't resent it; I just worried that I was missing something.

By then I had learned a lot about true success, true mentorship, and true leadership, and I had identified the next area of focus for my personal growth, courage. All those other things, when they lined up just right, were great. But where I faltered in them is where I had to walk in faith with courage and boldness. When I had the backing of business manuals and executives who agreed with my decisions and people who told me I was right, I could be bold. But when courage called me to go against the tidal wave of public opinion, or to face a giant, that's where I struggled.

So I looked at the biggest source of angst in my life, my schedule, and decided to make a courageous move, trusting, in faith, that God would honor my intentions. I worked on my plan over the weekend; then Monday morning each employee of Bellows International opened their e-mail to a one-page missive from me, Taylor Bellows, that read as follows.

Dear valued Bellows employee:

The following is a directive from me, and I expect it to be followed without exception, starting this day.

Every employee will be permitted to work a flex schedule in order to live out personal priorities. For those dependent on tracking hours, you may submit a time sheet for hours you put in at home. Does this mean you can move your entire position to your home office? That is for you to decide, based on a balance between your family and personal needs and the job you have to do.

No employee of Bellows International will be permitted to work any hours on Sundays. This includes the creating and/or sending of e-mails.

It is my desire that you will work a proper business day, that you will put in your greatest effort during those hours, and that you will then return home, leaving work behind. In the morning please have breakfast with your family, stop for coffee with some friends, or get in some exercise. In other words, do not start work until you've cared for yourself and your loved ones.

Please take a one-hour paid lunch break each workday. In the evening every employee should hurry home as close to five o'clock as possible to enjoy his or her family or pleasurable activities. Please plan your day to ensure communication with our international business partners in a timely manner that does not entail late or extreme hours for yourself.

Life is too short to run yourself into exhaustion. Bellows International will crank on as it has been, or it won't. Either way it's up to God. It's not your job to give your life for this company.

For those of you who've been working as an hourly employee and are counting on those over-time hours, rest easy. The hours you've been paid over the last year will be averaged, and that number will become your new salary for your forty-hour workweek.

While your feedback is always appreciated, this decision has been made. My secretary will not be putting through negative calls or e-mails on this issue. Thank you for your support and your continued dedication to Bellows International and to me.

Taylor Bellows

p.s. As a personal note, I have no doubt in my mind that God has a plan for each of you and for this company. I don't believe that his plan includes sixty-hour workweeks. I believe God will bless this company and your families with this new commit-ment to balance.

Brendan shut the book and looked at each of his friends. What did they think? Doug could barely close his mouth from his shock. Andy nodded with a big grin on his face. Sam looked doubtful yet hopeful.

Doug shook his head. "That was true courage."

"Oh, yeah. It sure was. God had to do work in Taylor before he arrived at that point. But once he got there…" Brendan smiled.

"He called me that night," Andy said. "I helped him write that e-mail and prayed for him and his company while the changes were taking place." He heaved a leg over the stool and sat down, his elbows on the island.

"See? That's why it took all four of us to hold him up adequately. If he'd have come to me for advice about that, I'd have convinced him he was crazy." Doug's eyebrows furrowed. "I'd have been wrong."

"So how did it turn out?" Sam asked.

Brendan shrugged and lifted the book. "You want to hear more? I haven't read past here yet."

Sam nodded. "Yeah. Definitely."

I had to laugh when I sent that e-mail at 8:02 on Monday morning. I knew my secretary was in for a long day of phone calls and e-mails from everyone at manager level and above. They were striving for bonuses. They were working toward sales goals and figures, and to tell them they were losing hours each week had to be scary for them. It was scary for me. I knew how many families depended on their incomes and how many people's lives I was affecting by my decision, not to mention my own. It could have blown up in my face.

But I had committed to this choice, not for the blessing on the bottom line, not so my employees could keep their kids clothed in designer duds. That wasn't the point. I committed to my decision because God told me to. He called me to a place of higher living and asked me to inspire others to that place. What choice did I have?

At first my plan looked like a failure. It looked bleak. Numbers went down for the month, then the quarter. A few people quit the company because they felt I had crippled them and prevented them from achieving success. But as with any sweeping drastic change, there was going to be some adjustment. I knew that going in.

Then the pendulum swung the other way. Sales numbers began to climb and climb and climb. Our insurance costs dropped as people became healthier. Families were restored where divorce had seemed inevitable. And the overall culture in the hallways, the break rooms, and the cafeteria was one of peace and joy. Balance had come to our company and therefore to the lives of the employees.

Which gave me another idea. So I sent a new memo.

Chapter Seven
TRUE TRANSFORMATION

"Can you pass me the tape?" Brendan held the flap of the box closed while Ann reached for the roll then tossed it to him.

"I can't believe we'll be walking out of here today, never to return." Ann dusted her hands on her pants and turned in a full circle, taking in the sight of their Midtown Manhattan apartment. Brendan remembered the day they'd found it—all that searching, high-rise after high-rise, until they walked into this place.

They could have upgraded in recent years, but why? The place was fully remodeled, had bright lights, and was high above the hustle and bustle of New York City but close enough to enjoy the city they loved. It was perfect. And now someone else would be calling it home.

They were moving on to bigger and better things.

"So when do the first families arrive at the ranch?" Ann said, returning to her taping.

"Oh, not for a month."

"Phew! I was afraid you were going to say 'Next week.' We have a lot to do there before they show up."

"No, definitely not next week. I've got to get the horses ready and get some trails prepared. I've got to stock up on wood and build that zip line we've been talking about." Brendan smiled. "I've sure got my work cut out for me."

"Oh, yeah. That's for sure." Ann shook her head. "You know I'll help, but there's a limit to what I can do."

"You can cook, right?" Brendan winked.

"Yeah, that I can do. It'll sure be nice to have a bunch of people to cook for. I keep envisioning happy people running into my kitchen after burning all their energy outside. I want to pile their plates full of good food to nourish their bodies so they'll trust us to let God's word nourish their souls."

Brendan nodded. "That's what it's all about, love."

"Especially when it's food they've helped grow and cultivate. Honey from our beehives. Vegetables from our gardens. Meat from our pasture. Unbelievable." Ann sighed in complete contentment.

"Just as God designed it." Brendan scribbled "kitchen stuff" on the box he'd just sealed.

"There. I think this is the last box." Ann pulled open the closet door. "Yep, empty."

"Hey, babe?"

And slipped an arm around his waist and gazed up. "What?"

"Would you mind going down and making sure the movers are taking care of things? I have some stuff I need to do up here alone."

Ann looked deep into his eyes. "You bet, love. I'll see you downstairs when you're ready." She stood in the doorway, her hands on the frame, as she glanced around the apartment they'd called home for twenty years. She blinked a few times then gave a swift nod before she turned and left.

What a strong woman. She always had been. Stronger than Brendan, for sure.

He strode to his favorite window. The leather chair was gone. The rich draperies were gone. But the heartbeat of the city thriving beyond the glass still beat on.

He pulled out *The Summary*. "Taylor, our last opportunity to share some words here in this place. I've read this journal over and over, and I've learned more about you and more about myself each time. One of these days, I'm going to start on the other books, but this one volume has been almost more than I could handle until now."

Brendan flipped to his favorite part.

How does it feel to succeed at business but fail with your own son?

Allison and I repaired our marriage and then decided it was time for us to be parents. It was kind of a snap decision offered to us by a pediatrician friend of ours—a closed adoption of a ten-year-old boy. We never got all the details of the story because of the privacy clause. All we knew—all we really needed to know—was that God had dropped the opportunity for us to be parents right into our laps long after we'd decided not to.

As an aside, it was hard to watch Brendan and Ann strive so hard to have a child and always come up empty. Allison and I knew we could have children; we just didn't want them. It's hard to write that, to realize that our lack of desire for children was birthed only from pure selfishness. I guess that's OK and better than bringing a child into an unstable family, but it felt shallow.

Ouch. Even though Brendan was way past the suffering that came from never being able to have children of his own, the words still stung. Ann had dealt with it better than he had in those early years, and she had, of course, been a source of great comfort for Brendan. Maybe she'd held out for an Abraham-Sarah miracle. Maybe that's what the ranch was, in a way.

By the time Ann had started to feel hurt by the childless bedrooms, it was Brendan who had turned a corner and found his. So, for once, he'd been able to lift his wife in her weakness.

Why hadn't God given them children? Brendan didn't know. On paper it sure seemed like a divine mistake. One day he would find out the answer to their question. In the meantime he'd trust that God had made the right choice.

So there we were with the gift of this ten-year-old boy who needed a mom and dad. We were ready.

Logan moved into our home and our hearts. Our blessings were full.

Over the years I did what I could to be a great dad. I gave him time, love, attention, and training for life and love. I really thought I had done well. And I know Allison was an awesome mom. No surprise there.

I don't know what happened, but one day Logan turned on me. He said all kinds of hateful things and stormed out of the house. He said he wanted nothing to do with Allison or me because we weren't his parents. He said God was a myth, and he wanted nothing to do with religion. He rejected who we were and where he came from. He rejected us.

Nothing in my life could have felt as bad as that moment.

Months went by. A year went by. Another year went by. I'm embarrassed to admit that by then I had lost track of where Logan had moved. He'd always been on the go, looking for some kind of answers. Part of me believed he'd find them or give up the search and come home. The other part of me got used to the idea that he might never return.

But I prayed. Allison and I prayed every single day for his safety and his return. And we prayed that God would get a hold of his heart.

One day I got a call that Logan was in the hospital and needed emergency surgery. He'd been in an accident and had internal damage. I discovered he needed blood, but due to his special blood type, neither Allison nor I could offer assistance. I felt like a failure again. My son lay there in the hospital, needing me, and I couldn't meet his need.

But Brendan could. I called my best friend and begged; actually I think I pretty much ordered him to come to the hospital immediately and help my son.

Bren hung up the phone without even saying goodbye. I knew he was on his way.

Allison and I raced to the hospital and practically bumped into Brendan at the entrance. On our way up, we found the doctor and took the steps to get Logan what he needed.

When my boy awoke from surgery, I noticed some of his anger had faded. He cracked a smile within moments of being awake and even made a little joke. A few hours later, he was making small talk with Allison and me as though nothing had happened.

But the next day...the next day was when he told us he was sorry. He allowed the tears to fall freely as he apologized for the hurt he'd put us through. Then he told me he'd assumed we could never open our hearts or our home to him again after he had rejected us so brutally.

I looked at Allison, and we laughed.

I grabbed Logan's hand. "Oh, my sweet son," I said, "from the moment I laid eyes on you, I was yours. I will take as much of you as you're willing to share with me, and I never will resent you for the part you hold back. What I have is yours always and completely. You never will find a closed door to our hearts and our home. Will you come home, son?"

Logan nodded. "I love you, Dad."

"I love you too, Son."

For some people the journey takes a lifetime. It sure did for me. My lessons were hard won. The journey from selfishness and depravity to my total transformation took almost my entire life.

For Logan it was different. The minute he made the decision to return as a prodigal son back to the fold of our home, he shed the trappings of the world and embraced truth. He gave his heart to Christ on day one, and by day two, he was witnessing to other people and signing up for mission trips at church. He jumped all in and never looked back. Today he is making a difference in the lives of people as the pastor of his own church.

My son, the pastor.

Ah. Brendan glanced up from the words on the page and looked through the window, down the street. The spire that always reminded Brendan of Logan's inner-city church stood proudly, pointing to the heavens—a testimony of God's faithfulness.

Brendan closed his eyes. True transformation. Taylor had taken a long time to arrive at his, but it was powerful and had affected the lives of hundreds, if not thousands, of people. Logan saw his life transformed by God in a matter of moments. It was miraculous and continued to touch the lives of many, many people.

But Brendan? Well, it seemed his true transformation had only just begun.

He smiled at his reflection in the window. He'd walked with God his whole life. Since he was a little boy, he'd been an example to others and tried to please Jesus with his choices and his behavior. He loved his wife and his friends. And his God. He didn't think he needed a transformation…until he read Taylor's book. It was here, in these pages. When Brendan looked down at the journal and thumbed through the handwritten words, he learned what true transformation really was.

God calls us to power living, Brendan realized. It's not about racking up good deeds and years of service; it's about surrender. It's in the moment of surrender that true transformation begins. At the end of the day, one thing is certain. We are all broken. From the beginning until now, we are a broken people living in broken bodies. What God offers is life, now and eternally. While inward transformation happens suddenly, the outward expression of that change is a gradual process that comes about when we fully surrender.

It is that complete surrender that draws us closer to the one who saved us. A transformed life looks different. It is a life *connected* to others in a meaningful way that makes a difference. A transformed life *serves* others in a way that strengthens the body of Christ and spreads his word. And a transformed life *shares* with others; these transformed people share their resources, time, money, and energy, but mostly they share their stories. A transformed life leads to a transformed world.

Taylor had figured it out before Brendan had. How was that even possible? But isn't that the mark of a great leader? To mentor and inspire others to greater things than he, himself, has ever known? Now it was Brendan's turn to live a truly transformed life and share it with others.

He moved from the window and stooped to tuck the journal into his bag. A slip of paper fluttered to the floor. "What's this?" He bent to pick up the folded square of lined yellow paper.

Bren—
Do me a favor? Publish a book. Tell people this stuff. It's important.

Love,
God, by way of his vessel, Taylor Bellows, II

Chapter Eight
THE FINAL STORY

"So, Dean, you brought your family here to the B2B ranch for a long family vacation, right?" Brendan ducked to avoid a branch that stuck out in the path. He'd have to come back with clippers to get rid of that one. "I'll bet you got some resistance when you told the family what you were doing."

"Yep. We've been here for a little over two weeks." Dean looked up and locked eyes with Brendan's. "It was the best decision I ever made, but I definitely caught some flack for it. My daughter Tracy wanted to lie on a beach. Seth wanted to stay home—vacations require too much togetherness for him. And Leslie wanted to go shopping in New York City."

"It's impressive that you stood your ground and got the family here. How'd you do it?"

Dean shrugged. "There comes a point when a man has to defend what's his. It was time to take my family back or lose them forever."

Amen. "I'm so glad you did. And now, as you know, one of the main focuses of your time here takes place in these next two weeks—some counseling, debriefing, and forward thinking." Brendan stopped walking and turned to face Dean. "Man, the most important thing is that you identify the principles of being a difference maker then intentionally apply them to all areas of your life. If you do that, your time here will be worth everything. If you don't, then…"

Dean nodded, his eyebrows furrowed. "We might as well have stayed at home, or worse, gone shopping."

Brendan shrugged. "I don't know about that, but you'd definitely miss out on the fullness of the plan God had for you this summer. You see, it's one thing to unearth your weaknesses and lay them before the cross. It's another to work through your relationship struggles to find and offer forgiveness to family members. It's yet another to renew your commitment to working together on relationships and moving forward in your relationship with God. But none of that tells you *how* to do it. That's what these next two weeks are for."

Dean nodded then stared at the top of his shoes. "That's what I'm afraid of. What if I can't do it? I mean, what about these people—people I love—who are so dependent on me to lead this family after we get home? They've learned all about surrender and family and relationships and even submission. My part as a husband, as a provider, as a father… There's just so much responsibility. What if I fail?"

"That's a really great question, Dean. I'm glad you asked it. Because you will fail. Absolutely, with complete certainty, I promise you, you will fail."

Dean snorted. "Well, in that case, I guess I'll be heading home now."

"No, I think you know what I'm talking about." Brendan turned as they continued their hike through the trees at the back of the B2B ranch. "So many men have wound up where you are—this moment of realization that ignorance is much easier than the responsibility that comes with the recognition of their true calling.

"You don't have the power in yourself to serve your family as God has called you to do it. In your own power, you'll battle for control, you'll fight for your rights, you'll check out when things get tough. But in God's power, you'll sacrifice for your loved ones, you'll do the hard work to teach and lead, and you'll serve with the heart of Christ, being an example of his love to those you uphold."

"That sounds so beautiful…and actually perfectly in line with God's character. But it's not *my* character. I know I'll have every intention to live that kind of life, in accordance with God's calling, but I'll grab the reins over and over and forget my true calling time and time again." Dean's shoulders slumped. "What then?"

"Ah. Where you are right now, brother, is our savior's favorite place for you to be. When you are weak, he is strong. When you're in need, you look to him. When you feel inadequate, he pours his complete fullness into you. It's only when you step back from yourself that you can see him clearly. It's painful now, but you're right—it's beautiful."

"OK, then what do you suggest I do?" Dean shot a glance at Brendan.

"Stay in *this* place." Brendan placed his palm on Dean's shoulder. "This place of humility and surrender. It's where you'll meet Jesus."

Hmm. That sounded great to Brendan, because he'd been on this road for a while, but Dean probably wanted more specifics. "Look, I'm going to walk you through the details in the coming days," Brendan said. "You and your family will be sitting down with me for a couple of hours a day over the next week. We'll go over all of this. As I talk with you about servant leadership, I'll be talking with them about forgiveness and surrender. Everyone has work to do."

Dean nodded. "That makes sense. I'm responsible for my part before God—for what he's called me to do. And they have their growing and learning and responding to do as well."

"Exactly." Brendan rubbed his chin. "You know, I have a question. If there's one thing, up to this point, that has made the biggest difference in your life during your stay at the ranch, what would you say it was?"

Dean looked up at the sky and exhaled. "Wow. That's a really hard question. I'd have to say, off the top of my head, the most life-changing thing is what I've learned about prioritizing. Nothing in itself is wrong. Working a job, being successful, having a full bank account—those things aren't wrong in themselves. But when that focus consumes a person's heart and mind, and people are pushed aside in the process, it's wrong. Those behaviors were destroying my family and eating us up from the inside out. It's all about godly priorities. Am I all in...or not?"

"Ah, yes. All in. We talk about that a lot here. What does it mean to you?"

"I suppose I might feel differently after we go through our talks, but right now I'd say that, for me, being all in means being open to whatever changes God wants to work in my life or my heart. It means hearing from him and doing the hard work to make the change, and allowing him to live in me and work through me."

Brendan brushed his hands across his shoulders and laughed. "Well, you can go now. My work here is done."

"Yeah, it sounds really good, but I'm not sure how to apply it to my life. I'm hoping you'll help me with that as we move on."

"You got it."

Chapter Nine
APPLICATION

"OK. Here we go." Brendan looked at Ann and smiled then turned back to the group. "This is our favorite part." He grabbed four copies of *The Difference Maker* and passed them around the circle. "The first thing I recommend you do is open your copy and write your name in the front. You're going to be making notes and applying everything you read to your own life, looking at your past and considering your future. This is personal."

He shifted in his seat to face Dean. "You're the leader, the husband, and the father. As we've already discussed, you have a certain set of jobs—responsibilities, if you will. Everything you read in this book will apply to you in a different way than it will to Leslie."

"Leslie." Brendan turned his gaze to the pretty redhead seated beside Dean. "You are the nurturer. Wife, mom, small business owner. You wear many hats and juggle many tasks. You're called upon to care for others, nurture and develop growth in your children, and lead in many areas of your life. What you read in this book will apply to your life much differently than it will to your children's lives."

Brendan turned to Seth and Tracy. "You guys are at a great moment in your lives. Everything you've done that you regret can be washed away. You can start anew and make a foundation for walking as a difference maker throughout the rest of your life. It's a beautiful place to be; you haven't made any marriage mistakes, business mistakes, or even parenting mistakes. What a privilege it is to be sitting here learning this now. Take it really seriously. It will change your life."

Ann stood up. "This afternoon we'd like you to find a quiet place to spend the next couple of hours and read Chapter One in your book. Pray for God to show you what he wants to teach you about true success." Ann moved to the door and smiled.

Brendan stood. "We'll meet back here tomorrow to go over what you read."

True Success

"All right, you've read through the first chapter in *The Difference Maker*. Now we're going to get into the heart of what true success is." Brendan leaned forward in his chair, his elbows resting on his thighs. "Dean, let's start with you. Before you came to the B2B ranch, how did you find true success?" He winked at Ann, who sat on the sofa beside Seth and Tracy. This was where it would all come together; it was Brendan's favorite part of the journey.

Dean drew in a deep breath then exhaled. "True success was all about promotions and raises and landing the next big deal. It was about buying fancy cars and paying for expensive vacations. It was about acquiring titles and things. It was all wrong."

Brendan nodded. "What about your kids? Where did they fit into your equation for success?"

"In my definition of true success? They didn't. That was Leslie's job. My identity was wrapped up in money and work." He shrugged. "After all I'm the man. I'm the breadwinner. I had to provide for my family. I just got a little caught up in it."

Leslie coughed.

Dean chuckled. "OK. Make that *a lot* caught up in it." He shook his head. "I can't believe how messed up my focus was."

Brendan nodded then turned to Leslie. "OK, your turn now. What was your definition of true success, Leslie?"

"Hmm. I guess being a successful woman, to me, meant wearing every hat available, along with the title of 'Superwoman.' " She looked down at her hands as she played with her wedding ring. "You know, if I could lead a Bible study at church, run a small business, raise my kids, run the parent organization at school, be in the band association, write a blog, et cetera, et cetera, I'd be a Superwoman. Then others would see me as the picture of self-sacrifice and that I had it all together. I guess that's how I saw true success."

Leslie looked at Dean and then her teenagers, her eyes brimming with tears. "Problem is, they didn't ask for all that stuff. So my attempt to be self-sacrificing was just a false front for a personal-identity search that left me feeling empty every time and striving for more and more of what I saw as success—all of which robbed my family of what they wanted most from me. And that was *me*."

Brendan nodded. She'd gotten it, as had Dean. What about the kids? "Seth, how about you? How does a teenage boy define true success?"

Seth cocked his head and ran his fingers through his brown curls. "Oh, dude. That's simple. A teenage boy defines true success by having a hot girlfriend. That's about it."

Tracy rolled her eyes and tossed back her sleek black hair. "Oh, give me a break. Like you've ever even had a girlfriend. You wouldn't know what to do with one if you did." She snapped her gum.

Seth jabbed Tracy in the ribs. "I'm not like you, Jezebel."

Tracy's jaw dropped open. "Mom, he called me that again."

"Well, if you stopped dating every boy in school, I guess I wouldn't have to." Seth sneered at his sister.

"Kids, you're being very rude." Leslie cast an apologetic glance at Brendan.

Dean shook his head and sighed.

Brendan laughed. *Teenagers will be teenagers,* he thought. But was there something to their jabs? "How about you, Tracy? What was true success to you before you came here?"

"Being popular?" Tracy shrugged. "I mean, a lot goes into that whole thing. Having the right clothes, having the right body shape, wearing the right makeup, having the right friends." She shook her head and chomped on the wad of gum. "It's not easy to have that kind of success."

"No, it sure isn't." Brendan shook his head and waited. She had more to say. He could feel it.

"But I guess I see that true popularity is the same thing as what this book says about true success. Doing what God has called me to do and being an example to others is more important than being liked. The popularity will come, or it won't. That has to be OK with me."

"Is it?"

The chomping stopped. "Is it OK with me?"

Brendan nodded. The answer to this question would determine Tracy's outcome.

"I guess mentally it's OK. I mean, I get it. I get what God wants for me and from me. And I want in on it. You know? I want to be the person he created me to be. But..." Tracy shrugged.

Brendan leaned forward. "What? But what?" She was so close.

"If I make some kind of commitment to live a different way... If I say that popularity in my school isn't important to me, or I say that having just the right boyfriend doesn't matter, then great. I'm sure I mean it for this hour. I'm sure my intentions are good. I know I mean it. Only I know what goes on inside of me."

Seth chuckled.

Leslie reached over and put her hand on Seth's thigh. She shook her head and held a finger to her lips.

"You're right, Tracy." Brendan nodded. "Only you know what your motivations and your intentions really are."

Tracy's eyes filled with tears. "But you know what else I know?"

Brandon waited.

Head down, Tracy wiped her eyes with a tissue. "I know that I'll mess up. I know it won't last."

Ah. There it was. The power struggle. Brendan stood to his feet. "Here's my question for you, actually for all of you. Are you willing to make a change?"

Tracy nodded. Her family followed.

"OK then. That's the first step. You take this step toward God in desire and commitment. He meets you there and empowers you through the journey." Brendan paced in front of them. "Yes! You *will* stumble. You *will* fall. We've been talking about that throughout your time here and the conversations we've been having. It's part of human nature. It's why we need a savior. In fact our weakness is what reveals God's strength. Through your surrender in the midst of your confusion and your frailty is where you will find him the most in your life—if you trust him."

Brendan took his seat. *Lord, please let these truths take hold.* He smiled at the group. "Great insight today, you guys. So what now? Looking back over your time here at the ranch and what you read in Chapter One of *The Difference Maker*, what is your definition of true success now?"

_____

_____

_____

_____

_____

_____

_____

_____

What does Jesus say about true success in the following verses?

"Whatever you do, do it as service to Him, and *He* will guarantee your success."
—Proverbs 16:3 (VOICE)

_____
_____
_____
_____
_____
_____
_____

"I am not saying this because I am in need, for I have learned to be content whatever the circumstances. I know what it is to be in need, and I know what it is to have plenty.
I have learned the secret of being content in any and every situation, whether well fed or hungry, whether living in plenty or in want. I can do all this through him who gives me strength."
—Philippians 4:11–13

_____
_____
_____
_____
_____
_____
_____

"Blessed is the one who does not walk in step with the wicked or stand in the way that sinners take or sit in the company of mockers, but whose delight is in the law of the Lord, and who meditates on his law day and night. That person is like a tree planted by streams of water,

which yields its fruit in season and whose leaf does not
wither—whatever they do prospers."
—Psalm 1:1–3

_____

_____

_____

_____

_____

_____

_____

What are some of the things you'll have to change in your
life in order to find true success?

_____

_____

_____

_____

_____

_____

What do you think will be the biggest obstacles to making
those changes?

_____

_____

_____

_____

_____

_____

_____

How will you overcome those challenges on your road to true success?

_____

_____

_____

_____

_____

_____

_____

"Great! Now this is where we make the change happen." Brendan smiled. "If you're ready to make a commitment to the pursuit of true success, if you're *all in*, then pray the following prayer with me and sign your name below."

Heavenly Father, please forgive me for chasing so hard after the things the world has dangled in front of me. Whether it's money or notoriety, or popularity and relationships, help me to remember what's really important and to invest my life into the kingdom and into your work. Give me a small glimpse of the way you see me so I truly can feel success on my journey. Guide my steps as I navigate this life in pursuit of your will for me, true success. Amen.

Signed: _____

_____

True Mentorship

"So how did your reading go last night, gang?" Ann smiled as Dean, Leslie, Seth, and Tracy entered the study and settled into the overstuffed chairs.

"This was a hard one for me." Leslie flipped through the pages of her book then pointed at one. "Here. This part. Taylor said, 'Because when we stumble—and we *will* stumble—we need someone to pick us up. And in our daily lives, we need someone we can trust to hold us accountable as we grow, which I hope to never stop doing. I truly feel sorry for the soul who goes through life and has no one there for them. It has been a blessing for me to be there for others.'"

Brendan nodded and grinned. "Right. Isn't that awesome?"

Leslie sighed. "I don't know about 'awesome.' I mean, I don't have a relationship like that. And even if I did, I don't know that I could be truly honest and accountable. How could I do that? Lay it all out there, and trust another human being not only to continue to love me without judging me, but also to continue to see the good stuff after my sin and doubt and fear have been revealed?"

Brendan nodded. Wow. This family was so insightful, so ready. *Lord, help me know what to say.*

"You know…" Dean stood to his feet and walked to the window. "I couldn't really put my finger on what bothered me about this chapter, but I think that's it. I think it's the concept of surrendering in complete honesty to someone else. Maybe it's actually harder to be mentored than is it to be a mentor."

Brendan smiled at Ann then looked back to the group. "Everyone is at a different place at different times. There's always someone behind you who needs to be mentored by you, and someone ahead of you who can pull you forward on the journey. It's a perfect plan, if you submit to it."

"That's what I'm saying." Leslie sighed. "If I submit to it. How can I do that? How can I know I'll be completely honest?"

"Really, it's just a matter of trusting that God will make it clear when the time is right and who your accountability partners and mentors should be. Once you make yourself available for those connections, he'll send them to you in his timing." Brendan smiled. "Trust. It's not all on *you* to make this thing happen. It's only on you to make yourself available. A willing servant and vessel."

Leslie nodded. "That makes sense."

"And," Dean spoke hesitantly, "what about that whole thing about the Mighty Three? I haven't really had time for friends over these recent years. I've been so busy with work that I let many of personal relationships die. I trust God, like you say, but what should I do in the meantime?"

Brendan looked deep into Dean's eyes. *Fear*. It was understandable. What if a person had to walk the journey alone? Brendan knew he sure wouldn't want to. But Dean didn't have to—at least not for long. "Here's what you do. You pray every day that God will send solid godly friends into your life. You pray that he'll show you who those people are and then give you the tools you need to cultivate those friendships. It takes work and intentionality. You have to make yourself available and then chase after those relationships. Not only will people come up alongside you and mentor you, but you'll also discover people you can reach."

Leslie lifted a hand. "I have somewhat of the opposite problem. I have so many friends. Bible study groups, school groups, and people I stayed in touch with from college, even high school. People I try in keep up with online. How do I prioritize those relationships? What if I miss an opportunity to mentor someone just because they're on the outskirts of my radar?"

Tracy leaned forward. "Yeah. That makes a lot of sense. How do we figure that out?"

Brendan chuckled. "I'm going to let Ann handle this one. This is usually more of a women's issue than a men's problem."

Ann smiled. "Yeah, you don't see many guys dealing with the problem of having too many friends. It seems clear that many, if not most, of your relationships are on the surface, Leslie, even your Bible study friends. Now what you need to do is find the people who are all in—people who uphold your choices and support your family."

Ann looked up at the ceiling for a moment. "Here. Let me give you example. If you're going out to dinner once a month with your college friends to stay in touch and keep up with their families, that, in itself, isn't a problem. But if those people spend the entire evening complaining about their spouses and married life, it might not be the most productive way to spend your evening."

Leslie smirked. "Yeah, I see what you mean. Some of my friends use prayer-request time as a gossip opportunity and a husband-bashing session. I probably don't want to pour my deepest truths out in that environment."

"Not at all. You want to surround yourself with people who'll build you up and exhort you toward godly living. People who'll encourage you to honor your husband and model godly behavior before your children. People who'll be honest with you when you're messing up. Those are true friends and mentors."

"Yeah, I totally get what you're saying, and that makes perfect sense," Leslie said. "But what about the people I need to mentor? How do I sift through all those people and figure out who God wants me to pour my effort into?"

Brendan glanced at Dean. "Can you give this one a shot, Dean?"

Dean's head jerked back in surprise. "I guess so. Yes. I mean, of course I can." He bit his lip for a moment. "The deal is, like we've been learning, we have to trust the power of prayer and the discernment we get from the Holy Spirit. When you question who God has for you to mentor, you have to trust that he'll show you. Maybe the need will jump out to you from an e-mail or a phone call. Or maybe someone will come to you directly and ask for help. Maybe it hasn't been clear until now, because you haven't been ready until now." Dean sat back heavily, almost as though the effort had exhausted him. But the thrill was evident on his face.

"There you go." Brendan beamed. *Leadership at its finest.* "So let's all turn to our journals." Brendan paused until everyone found the right spot. "First of all, identify some names of people on the journey ahead of you. People you look up to. Mentors."

_____

_____

_____

_____

_____

_____

_____

Of those names, circle the three that stand out to you for some reason as being good examples of godly living. They have a strong prayer life; they have a powerful knowledge of the word of God. List them here.

_____
_____
_____
_____
_____

Could they be your Mighty Three?

_____
_____
_____
_____
_____
_____
_____

Now look back. Who is coming up behind you who may be in need of a mentor for this part of his or her own journey?

_____
_____
_____
_____
_____
_____
_____

Ann cleared her throat. "If no names come to mind right away, pray and ask God to show you whom he has for you to mentor. As you saw from Taylor's experience, someone is always there. No matter what stage you're at in life, there's someone behind you."

Brendan stood up and reached for his Bible. "Now for the hard part. Accountability. You're right, Leslie. It's a hard concept. Many people never fully embrace it. But let's see what the Bible says about it. What do these verses from Scripture mean to you?"

"Likewise, teach the older women to be reverent in the way they live, not to be slanderers or addicted to much wine, but to teach what is good. Then they can urge the younger women to love their husbands and children, to be self-controlled and pure, to be busy at home, to be kind, and to be subject to their husbands, so that no one will malign the word of God."
—Titus 2:3–5

_____
_____
_____
_____
_____
_____
_____

"As iron sharpens iron, so one person
sharpens another."
—Proverbs 27:17

_____
_____
_____
_____
_____
_____
_____

"Be shepherds of God's flock that is under your care, watching over them—not because you must, but because you are willing, as God wants you to be; not pursuing dishonest gain, but eager to serve; not lording it over those entrusted to you, but being examples to the flock. And when the Chief Shepherd appears, you will receive the crown of glory that will never fade away."
—I Peter 5:1–4

_____
_____
_____
_____
_____
_____
_____

"In the same way, you who are younger, submit your-selves to your elders. All of you, clothe yourselves with humility toward one another, because,
'God opposes the proud but shows favor to the humble.'
"
—I Peter 5:5

_____
_____
_____
_____
_____
_____
_____

What are your thoughts about accountability and what scares you? Write your answers in the space provided, because one day you'll look back and remember how you felt. Remembering your feelings will help you mentor others at the start of their journeys.

_____
_____
_____
_____
_____

Brendan grinned. "Are you all in and ready to make a commitment to true mentorship? If so, say the following prayer with me, and then sign your name.

Father, you have created a beautiful picture of mentorship. Help me pour into the people who are coming up behind me who need my insight and my help on their journey. Help me see their need and then meet it in whatever way you would have me reach them. Give me the grace to see the beauty within each person, just as you have seen it in me. And then, Lord, help me surrender to accountability, and help me be honest with myself as much as I'm honest with them. Forgive me for my shortcomings, and guide me into true mentorship. Amen.

Signed : _____

_____

True Leadership

"I have a question about leadership." Seth sloughed into the study, his pants dragging on the floor.

Brendan lifted his head and closed his Bible. "Yes, Seth? What can I help you with?" He gestured for the rest of Seth's family to take a seat.

"Well, to be a leader, do I have to dress like some business guy or get a job at some company? I mean, I can't see myself doing that kind of thing. I want to fix motorcycles… maybe even race them. But is God saying I'm not a leader if I don't do something big like my dad?"

"Oh, Seth." Brendan felt his eyes sting. There was so much more behind that question than Seth was letting on—so much more doubt and insecurity behind his casual, carefree exterior than he wanted his parents, or even Brendan and Ann, to see. But that didn't mean Brendan couldn't speak to it. "Seth, Jesus has a message for you. Guess what, brother? He loves you—exactly how you are, even with your pants dragging on the floor."

Everyone laughed.

"With that piercing in your nose. With your wild hairdo. He loves you just exactly the way you are. And the cool part is that there are people who will *only* look to someone like you for leadership. Someone who understands them. Someone who gets where they've been and where they want to go. Someone who knows what it feels like to be perceived as different."

Seth gaze cast down to the floor.

Bingo.

Brendan leaned forward with his elbows on his knees and looked into Seth's eyes. "I want you to know right now—no, *Jesus* wants you to know right now—that you are perfect exactly how you are. You are no more different from me than I am from your dad and than he is from Ann. Each of us was created with a completely unique set of talents and gifts and callings. Each of us has a personal journey to walk that is completely different than every single other person's on this planet."

Seth raised his gaze to meet Brendan's and nodded.

"We are all different. Equally. That's what makes us exactly the same in God's eyes. Worthy. Loved." Brendan looked a little deeper. "OK?"

A broad smile spread across Seth's face. "Yeah, man. It really is OK."

Brendan shifted his body toward Dean. "So how about you, Dean? How do feel about leadership now?"

He chuckled. "Well, like everything else I've been learning in the weeks I've been here at the ranch, I had it all wrong. Leadership isn't being the boss. It isn't having tons of people report to you and depend on you. Leadership is basically inspiring other people to follow Jesus. At least that's what true leadership is."

"Fabulous." Brendan nodded. "A true leader stirs other people to greater things and helps them find true success—God's success, which comes from serving people like Jesus does. So let's take a look at leadership, as we have with the other transformational truths we've been looking at. Related to true leadership, what do you see in your life that needs to change?"

_____
_____
_____
_____
_____
_____
_____

How will you go about changing these things? What obstacles do you see? How will you overcome these obstacles?

_____
_____
_____

_____
_____
_____
_____

If Jesus was the ultimate leader, what does the following verse from Scripture say about his submission to
leadership?

"Father, if you are willing, remove this cup from me.
Nevertheless, not my will, but yours, be done."
—Luke 22:42

_____
_____
_____
_____
_____
_____
_____

As Taylor shared, there are three good questions to ask
yourself on a regular basis. How would you answer these
today?

Who am I?

_____
_____
_____
_____
_____
_____
_____

Where am I going?

_____
_____
_____
_____

How am I going to get there?

_____
_____
_____
_____
_____
_____
_____

What do the following passages from Scripture say to you about true leadership?

"Keep watch over yourselves and all the flock of which the Holy Spirit has made you overseers. Be shepherds of the church of God,
which he bought with his own blood."
—Acts 20:28

_____
_____
_____
_____
_____
_____
_____

"Be shepherds of God's flock that is under your care, watching over them—not because you must, but

because you are willing, as God wants you to be; not pursuing dishonest gain, but eager to serve."
—I Peter 5:2

"Jesus knew that the Father had put all things under his power, and that he had come from God and was returning to God; so he got up from the meal, took off his outer clothing, and wrapped a towel around his waist. After that, he poured water into a basin and began to wash his disciples' feet, drying them with the towel that was wrapped around him."
—John 13:3–5

"When he had finished washing their feet, he put on his clothes and returned to his place. 'Do you understand what I have done for you?' he asked them. 'You call me Teacher and Lord, and rightly so, for that is what I am. Now that I, your Lord and Teacher, have washed your feet, you also should wash one another's feet. I have set you an example that you should do, as I have done for you."
—John 13:12–15

Brendan stood. "How about it? Are you all in on true leadership? Are you ready to make a commitment to be a servant leader? If so, pray the following prayer along with me and sign your name below."

Jesus, servant of all, please teach me to be a humble leader like you. Help me lay aside my own goals and ambitions to focus more on inspiring others to chase their dreams and live for you. Help me serve my family, my friends, and others in your name. Amen.

Signed: _____

_____

True Courage

"All right. Let's jump in and get started right away. Courage is a huge topic we can apply to every area of our lives." Brendan took a seat in his usual chair.

Ann sighed. "Wow. I really think Taylor was such a great example of this, as he made really difficult business decisions in his commitment to be all in. He pursued true courage that honored Jesus Christ by sacrificing the rewards of the world." She looked around the circle. "I wonder if any of you are dealing with a decision or a struggle that makes the concept of true courage a scary one. Would anyone like to share?"

Tracy raised a tentative hand. "I've got something."

Ann nodded as if she'd expected it. "Please, Tracy. The floor is yours."

"Well, I don't know if you realize how much things have changed for teenagers. Schools are full of pressure and bullying and popularity struggles. It's crazy what we have to deal with. If we don't follow the crowd, we'll stand out, and that'll make life a living hell. Sorry, but that's the only word I can come up with. How can Jesus ask me to do that?"

Ann glanced at Brendan, who nodded. "Go on."

"Well, Tracy," Ann began, "those are excellent points. There are several things I'd like to address here, if you don't mind. First of all, the concept that things have changed and there's more peer pressure and popularity struggles today than there was when I was younger. I'm sorry, but it's just not true. Yes, schools are different in that kids might be experiencing things at a younger age now than they did then, and parents are allowing them to get away with more than they did in my high school years. But sin is sin, and it doesn't change. In fact the Bible tells us there's nothing new under the sun. Nothing at all."

Tracy shrugged. She opened her mouth as if to speak, then snapped it shut.

"I know you're not buying it," Ann told her. "I get that. But regardless of whether the rest of us in this room are out of touch or not, your concerns are valid. They're your reality, and what you're asking is how Jesus can call you to true courage if it'll cost you your happiness and your friendships. Right?"

"Exactly." Tracy stared at the floor. "By standing up against the crowd or against peer pressure one time, I can turn my existence at high school from a happy one to a devastating, miserable one in, like, seconds. I don't know if I've got it in me to go through that for two more years."

Ann nodded. "I understand. So do your parents. In fact Jesus does too. He said the road is never easy when we choose to follow him. But he does call us to walk that hard road. The great thing is that he's there with you. Whatever sufferings you may endure in this world are so temporary, so miniscule compared to the eternal rewards you'll receive from God in heaven when you stand up and defend his name."

Brendan cleared his throat and leaned in. "Tracy, I believe you're called to do great things for the kingdom. I think we can all see that."

Dean and Leslie nodded.

"Definitely." Ann smiled.

Seth rolled his eyes and slouched lower in his seat.

Brendan placed his hand on Tracy's shoulder and looked into her eyes. "You have to overcome this hurdle of fear. It will be through prayer and surrender, and the choice to be all in, that the pressures of the world and the trappings of popularity will fall away in unimportance as the fullness of the Holy Spirit consumes your life. Surrender comes first, then the freedom follows. I promise you—when you allow that to happen, it will not be a difficult choice."

Tracy nodded.

"Right," Ann said. "I think Taylor was a great example of that. Look at how much he had to lose, yet he said, 'I don't care. I won't sacrifice my calling and the surpassing greatness of following Jesus Christ for one more moment of worldly success.' Or popularity, as in your case, Tracy."

Brendan nodded. "So whether it's in business decisions, personal choices, lifestyle decisions, family commitments, or anything else God puts in your path for you to overcome

with true courage, he will make a way for you to do it."
Brendan raised his eyebrows.

"I get it. It's a step of faith." Tracy clenched her jaw.
"I have to just do it, just let go."

"Precisely." Brendan beamed. "So, as we have with
the other transformational truths we've been looking at,
let's take a look at courage. What do you see in your life
related to true courage that needs to change? What hard
thing is the Holy Spirit laying on your heart right now?"

_____

_____

_____

_____

_____

_____

_____

What obstacles do you see? And how will you overcome
these obstacles?

_____

_____

_____

_____

_____

_____

_____

How do the following passages from Scripture help you
strive toward true courage?

"Have I not commanded you? Be strong and courageous. Do not be frightened, and do not be dismayed,
for the Lord your God is with you wherever you go."
—Joshua 1:9

_____

_____

_____

_____

_____

_____

_____

"So we say with confidence, 'The Lord is my helper;
I will not be afraid. What can mere mortals do to me?'
Remember your leaders, who spoke the word of God
to you. Consider the outcome of their way of life and
imitate their faith. Jesus Christ is the same yesterday and
today and forever."
—Hebrews 13:6–7

_____

_____

_____

_____

_____

_____

_____

"Finally, be strong in the Lord and in his mighty power.
Put on the full armor of God, so that you can take your
stand against the devil's schemes. For our struggle is not
against flesh and blood, but against the rulers, against
the authorities, against the powers of this dark world,
and against the spiritual forces of evil in the heavenly

realms. Therefore put on the full armor of God, so that when the day of evil comes, you may be able to stand your ground, and after you have done everything, to stand."
—Ephesians 6:10–13

_____
_____
_____
_____
_____
_____
_____

Brendan stood. "How about it? Are you all in on true courage? Are you ready to make a commitment to living boldly and doing the hard things in the name of Jesus? If so, pray the following prayer along with me then sign your name below."

Jesus, make me bold. Make me strong and mighty in your power that I can stand against the schemes of the devil and withstand the pressures of this world. Let me stand firm, confident in your word, and resolute in my determination to walk in true courage, no matter the cost. Help me apply true courage to my mentorship relationships, to my leadership style, and to my own successes. And finally, Lord, let my courage never bring glory to my name, but may it always point others to you. Amen.

Signed: _____

_____

True Transformation

"Transformation. Wow. What a concept." Brendan looked Dean in the eyes then moved to Leslie. Tracy nodded when his gaze moved to her, and Seth offered a smile in return. "I see a transformation on each of your faces. It's a beautiful thing." He grinned. "Now Ann is going to read to us from Taylor's words."

Ann smiled as she picked up *The Difference Maker* and flipped it open to her bookmarked page.

> *God calls us to power living. It's not about racking up good deeds and years of service; it's about surrender. In the moment of surrender, true transformation begins.*
>
> *At the end of the day, one thing is certain. We are all broken. From the beginning until now, we are a broken people living in broken bodies. What God offers is life, now and eternally. While inward transformation happens suddenly, the outward expression of that change is a gradual process that comes about when we fully surrender.*
>
> *It is that complete surrender that draws us closer to the one who saved us. A transformed life looks different. It is a life connected to others in a meaningful way that makes a difference. A transformed life serves others in a way that strengthens the body of Christ and spreads his word. And transformed lives share with others. They share their resources—time, money, and energy—but mostly they share their stories. A transformed life leads to a transformed world.*

"Thanks, love." Brendan patted his wife on the thigh. "Now let's look a bit deeper, as we have with the other transformational truths we've been discussing. How have you seen your own transformation unfold?"

_____

_____

_____

_____

_____

_____

_____

What do you love about it?

_____

_____

_____

_____

_____

_____

What scares you?

_____

_____

_____

_____

_____

_____

How will you share your transformation with others?

_____

_____

_____
_____
_____
_____
_____

What do the following passages fro Scripture mean to you
when you consider true transformation?

"Do not conform to the pattern of this world, but be
transformed by the renewing of your mind. Then you
will be able to test and approve what God's will is
—his good, pleasing and perfect will."
—Romans 12:2

_____
_____
_____
_____
_____
_____

"Therefore, if anyone is in Christ, the new creation has
come: The old has gone, the new is here!"
—2 Corinthians 5:17

_____
_____
_____
_____
_____
_____

"And whatever you do, whether in word or deed, do it
all in the name of the Lord Jesus, giving thanks to God
the Father through him."
—Colossians 3:17

_____

_____

_____

_____

_____

_____

"Being confident of this, that he who began a good work
in you will carry it on to completion until the day of
Christ Jesus."
—Philippians 1:6

_____

_____

_____

_____

_____

_____

How does Taylor's relationship with his son reflect the
way the Heavenly Father feels about you?

_____

_____

_____

_____

_____

_____

How does that motivate you?

_____

_____

_____

_____

_____

_____

_____

"So…are you all in?" Brendan locked eyes with each family member.

One by one they nodded.

"What if there's a cost? Are you willing to pay the sacrifice?"

"Yes. No matter what." Tracy grinned.

"We are." Dean held up Leslie's hand.

"Yeah. I'm in." Seth slumped in his chair.

"Wonderful." Brendan beamed. "Allow me to read this final prayer from Taylor's journal. It's a prayer for you."

Father God, I love the people who are reading these words with a passion that you birthed within me. Please use the words they've read and the commitments they've made to spur them on to true success. Help them serve others as true mentors and to allow themselves to submit to mentorship and accountability. And, Lord, let them walk in true leadership that they might inspire others to follow you. May true courage be the glue that holds it all together and gives them the strength to do the hard thing you put before them. Finally may they embrace true transformation that can only be found in you. Amen.

TONY BRIDWELL

Tony Bridwell is an international speaker, consultant, and coach for some of the largest organizations and their top leaders in the world. More than thirty years ago, Tony found his way from Oklahoma to the Dallas, Texas, area, where he and his wife Dee currently call home. With three children and two dogs, their life is a non-stop adventure. He is a frequent guest speaker at churches around the world when he isn't teaching Bible study at his local church. Tony will be the first to tell you he is where he is today because someone made a difference in his life along the way.

Made in the USA
San Bernardino, CA
06 January 2015